Praise for Reon Laudat's

It's a Love Thang

"Great plot and well-developed main characters. I loved the many humorous sections. They made for grand reading! Definitely recommended!"
—Huntressreviews.com

"A funny, well-written romp that is sure to delight. *It's a Love Thang* is a blast."
—*Romantic Times*

"Fresh…funny…charming."
—*Detroit Free Press*

"One of the finest contemporaries I've read all year. The smile and warm feelings I get from this book are reasons enough for me to give it two thumbs up…Isaiah and Ebony are really likeable, adorable characters."
—*Romance Novel Central*

More…

"*It's a Love Thang* is a funny ethnic romance…what makes the tale work is that different types of humor are employed from the subtle Benny-Carson looks to outright slapstick."

—thebestreviews.com

"A wild, roller-coaster ride…the competition between Ebony and Isaiah is fierce, surpassed only by their sizzling chemistry…a delightful romp…highly recommended."

—Cindy Penn of Wordweaving.com and
Midwest Book Reviews

"This is an author to watch…fun book…pretty fabulous characters…fans of romantic comedy will enjoy *It's a Love Thang*."

—*All About Romance*

"A fast-paced, high-energy adventure. Ebony and Isaiah are a likeable pair readers will warm to."

—*The Oakland Press*

"Very cute…enjoyable."

—*RAWSISTAZ*

What a Girl Wants

"Delightful!"

—*Romantic Times*

"Laudat has found an interesting balance of comedy and drama that works well and is sure to please all of her fans."

—*Romance in Color*

"Breezy…smart…sizzling…fast-paced."
—*The Oakland Press*

"Bright…sassy."

—*Detroit Free Press*

"Feisty! Highly recommended."

—Wordweaving.com

"By turns tender, funny, and very sexy."
—*Romance Junkies*

"Moving…thoroughly enjoyable."
—*A Romance Reader at Heart*

St. Martin's Paperbacks Titles
by Reon Laudat

If You Just Say Yes

It's a Love Thang

What a Girl Wants

Anthology

The Sistahood of
Shopaholics

Wanna Get
to
Know Ya

REON LAUDAT

St. Martin's Paperbacks

WANNA GET TO KNOW YA

Copyright © 2005 by Reon Laudat.

All rights reserved. No part of this book may be used or reproduced in any manner whatsoever without written permission except in the case of brief quotations embodied in critical articles or reviews. For information address St. Martin's Press, 175 Fifth Avenue, New York, NY 10010.

ISBN: 0-312-93414-9
EAN: 9780312-93414-9

Printed in the United States of America

St. Martin's Paperbacks edition/October 2005

St. Martin's Paperbacks are published by St. Martin's Press, 175 Fifth Avenue, New York, NY 10010.

10 9 8 7 6 5 4 3 2 1

To Peter and Christian,

with all my love

Acknowledgments

I'd like to thank:

My family and friends.

Jane Hankins, a real trucker chick, for getting me up to speed on the trucking life.

My editor, Monique Patterson, for her patience when deadlines loomed and my schedule got crazy.

Karyn Lewis and Sharon McCalop for being two of the nicest people I've had the pleasure of getting to know.

And last but not least, the readers.

Wanna Get
to
Know Ya

1

The Barracuda sat on muddy cement blocks next to a shabby white clapboard house..Despite years of rust and wear, the car was a welcome sight for C.J.'s road-weary eyes. She slammed on the brakes of her gray Dodge Dakota, screeching to a halt and double-parking beside a dusty blue Ford Escort with flat tires. She climbed out of her pickup and made her way to the Barracuda. Her fingertips slid along the rough surface of its trunk and side panels, then lingered at the metallic grille clouded by age and the elements. Peering through streaked and smudged windows, she caressed and patted its top. It needed plenty of TLC, but for C.J. it was love at first sight.

"Hot day-um!" C.J. stepped back and circled

the car three times, admiring its forward lean, rear spoiler, quarter-panel billboard decals, Rallye Red paint, and black interior.

She'd made a habit of perusing ads in local newspapers and magazines and on the Internet, searching for the make and model that matched the one on the crumpled page she'd ripped out of a *Muscle Car Madness* magazine ages ago.

At last! Finding her dream car after making a wrong turn off an interstate service drive, which led her down that sleepy cul-de-sac, was kismet. She stood there grinning, hugging herself, and staring at the car. A nosy old man working on his lawn next door had been watching C.J. since she got out of her truck. "Is something wrong, miss?" he called out to her.

"Everything's fine, Gramps, just fine." C.J. advanced up the cracked driveway. She knocked, all the while praying that the Barracuda's owner was home. She'd make him or her an offer that could not be refused. C.J. wouldn't leave until that baby was hers.

A young woman answered. She wore an impatient expression and a faded checkered print shift dress on her thin body and plastic pink curlers in her wheat blond hair. "Can I help you?" she asked through the ripped and puckered screen door.

"Um, yes," C.J. said. "About that car in the driveway. Is it yours?"

"Yeah? So?" The woman's suspicion and dismay were obvious as her sparse brows rushed together. "You from the city? Have the neighbors been complaining again? Don't worry; I was just about to take care of it. I have an interested buyer inside right now."

"No!" bolted out of C.J.'s mouth. "Please tell me you haven't closed the deal yet!"

The woman eyed C.J. curiously. "No? Why? Who are you?"

"Someone who is going to beat whatever offer is already on the table if you give me a chance," C.J. told her with complete confidence.

"Oh yeah?" The woman's shadowed gray eyes brightened with interest as she unlatched the screen door and cracked it open to invite C.J. inside her living room. She offered her guest a seat on a chair with a yellowed plastic covering. The thick scent of dinner—something fried—hung in the air.

C.J. immediately noticed the man seated on the adjacent chair to her right. *Ooh la la!* He looked as if he'd fallen off the pages of the *International Male* apparel catalogs she collected just to gawk at their fine-ass male models.

If she was absolutely sure this wasn't the woman's man and wasn't so focused on getting on her good side, C.J. might have taken more time appreciating just how incredibly studly the man was.

"*He* wants that ol' Barracuda, too." The woman gestured toward the hottie, who glared at C.J.

C.J. looked away from him and counted three kids. All but the one engrossed in a cartoon on the TV set turned curious eyes toward her.

"I'm C.J., by the way." She extended her hand for the woman to shake.

"Kathy, Kathy Bolen." Kathy curled her fingers around C.J.'s as she addressed the hunk. "C.J. here wants to make an offer on the car, too."

"Make an offer? But I thought we already had a deal," the man said evenly, though his strong, angular jaw appeared to clench.

Kathy flapped one hand dismissively, then shrugged at him. "But it's not final until sales documents are signed." She turned toward C.J. eagerly. "What are *you* willing to pay?"

Clearly exasperated, he interrupted, "So she just pops up outta nowhere—"

"Like you just popped up outta nowhere. So?" Kathy replied.

C.J.'s head snapped from Kathy to the other potential buyer, as if following the ball in a heated tennis match.

"But I thought we had a verbal agreement," he said.

"Ahhh, but we didn't shake on it," Kathy trilled, wagging an index finger at him.

He shot to his feet in a huff. "I didn't realize this would turn into an auction situation . . ."

C.J. took perverse satisfaction in his imminent departure. *Yeah! Go! Vamoose! Am-scray! Make like the wind and blow! Chop-chop! The car's mine, mine, mine!* She should've played it cool, because the expression on her face had obviously persuaded him to reconsider giving up. His dark eyes narrowed to slits as he pursed mighty sexy-looking lips in determination. C.J. silently chided herself. This was the enemy and he wasn't going to make getting the car that easy for her. It was not the time to get fixated on the man's world-class kisser and killer bod.

The glowering hottie pushed out an impatient sigh, then took his seat on the chair again, crossing his well-honed arms over a football field of a chest. He nailed C.J. with a determined appraisal that seemed to go on forever, causing her to squirm. He bit out, "On second thought . . ."

Kathy, of course, was thrilled at the idea of having two people so eager to purchase her car. Her expression turned stern again when she scolded the boy of no more than six sprawled belly first across the dingy beige carpeting. The adventures of Bugs Bunny and Elmer Fudd on the TV screen held him captive. "Bobby, didn't I tell you to turn off that damn TV and pick up your toys?"

Bobby peeled himself off the floor with a pout on his freckled face; then he gathered the toy trucks, cars, and spare racetrack parts scattered about the room.

A towheaded toddler wobbled over to cling to Kathy's dress tail. In the adjoining kitchen a sticky-faced baby was perched upon a high chair. The infant wailed and banged a goopy spoon against the tray to get Kathy's attention, to no avail.

"Tend to the kids first if you like," C.J. suggested.

"No, they can wait. Don't want to spoil 'em," Kathy replied instead.

C.J. inched to the edge of her chair as its plastic covering squeaked beneath her butt.

She and the hunk replied in unison: "Now about the car . . ."

The woman snorted and got real cozy on another chair or, rather, in the catbird seat. "And here I was thinking I had to shell out cash to have it towed away. The tires were stolen. I'm sure you noticed."

C.J. nodded. "The cement blocks kinda gave that away."

"That car was my inheritance from my father," Kathy added, grumbling under her breath. "The boozing bastard only caused Ma and me much grief when he was alive. Left Ma with a couple of ulcers, high blood pressure, and a stack of bills. Me? Got that thing in the driveway . . ." Her words trailed off when she realized she wasn't helping her own cause—as the seller—by revealing her disdain for the car and her dead daddy. She forced reverence into her tone. "But you know, now that I think about it, the car does have *some* sentimental value. It did belong to my daddy, flesh and blood and all."

"Is that right?" the hunk said, rolling his eyes skyward, obviously not buying Kathy's sudden flip-flop.

"I can't believe this day." Kathy faced the hunk. "You just show up on my doorstep 'cause one of my neighbors told you about the car." She then looked at C.J. "And then *wham*! A few minutes later you show up. Who'da thunk it? You both want the Barracuda, so go ahead." She settled back in her chair and crossed her bird legs as if she had all the time in the world. "Knock yourselves out. Make me an offer I can't refuse."

C.J. and the hunk eyeballed each other and squared off like old adversaries in a grudge match.

The fierce bidding ensued.

A few minutes later C.J. had prevailed. If she had held out for another Barracuda she'd have gotten a better deal. But she didn't want to wait any longer. Who knew if and when she'd even stumble upon another one? Tomorrow wasn't promised, and no one knew that better than C.J.

She'd paid more than the going price for similar cars in the same condition. After noting Kathy's mismatched thrift store furniture and her kids' ill-fitting clothing, C.J. had no regrets. Fortunately, the hunk backed off before she had to dip into her emergency reserve funds.

Before Kathy and C.J. could shake on the deal they'd struck, the hottie had stalked out of the house. C.J. obviously wanted the car more than he did, so she'd tamped down the twinge of guilt that surfaced for interrupting his transaction with Kathy. At last! She had her beloved Barracuda, and that was all that mattered.

2

C.J. stripped out of her clothing and stepped under a spray of hot water.

With a giddy grin still on her lips, she turned off the faucet and stepped out of the shower, wrapping a plush towel around her body. That old magazine photo of the Barracuda was taped to the bathroom mirror, now damp and clouded with steam. She tugged off the page and gazed longingly at the image of the car. Droplets from her hand and hair saturated the paper, but she didn't care. She brought the page to her lips and kissed it. "The last freakin' time I have to moon over a photo," she said out loud just as the doorbell rang.

C.J. moved from the bathroom to her bedroom, where she donned a white terry-cloth robe spread across her canopy bed. She grabbed a thick towel to drape around her shoulders. The doorbell rang again. "Coming! Damn!" She secured the belt to her robe, then dashed to the front door of her cozy ranch-style home. On the opposite side of the peephole she found her sister, Nina.

Save for the hair length and color, C.J. and Nina shared many physical features—the honeyed skin, the slim but curvy body, and large cappuccino-colored eyes. Most people assumed that they were identical twins instead of fraternal twins who were born six minutes apart. Nina, the older sister, got her peek at the world first.

C.J. used one hand to open the door and the other to rub the towel over soft waves that stretched about four inches down her back. Nina's hair would be just as long if she didn't have that standing appointment with a stylist who snipped and applied "sun" streaks to her tresses every two weeks. The result was a wild brown pixie cut with blond wisps that brought out the golden undertones of her skin. Most women who tried to pull off that particular helter-skelter do would look as if they'd barely survived the wrath of a garden shears–totin' psycho and lived to tell about it. But as with everything else, the look was edgy, hip, and perfect on C.J.'s sister. That day Nina sported a form-fitting denim jacket busy with sparkly appliqués, a brightly tie-dyed tube top, and low-slung jeans that hugged her flat lower tummy and long legs from hips to knees, then flared out to accommodate the platform sandals on her feet. In one hand she clutched a big pillow-like burst of purple feathers that functioned as a purse. Two romance novels, *Kiss Me Crazy* and *Passion's Gate*, peeked out of the purse's side pocket. In the other hand was a bag from Nordstrom, which had become a familiar accessory. Nina was a black-belt shopper at the top of her game, while C.J. had no use for Detroit's upscale malls. If she couldn't get it at Kmart or Costco, she didn't need it. Her wardrobe was heavy on flannel shirts in the fall and winter, T-shirts in the spring and summer, and all-season Wrangler jeans. She usually rocked the same clunky black boots year-round, too. No matter how blazing the temperature got outside. Thank God for the industrial-strength Dr. Scholl's Odor Eaters that managed to keep her feet from becoming biological weapons of mass destruction.

All that was missing was "the Elly May Clampett rope belt and the corked jug of moonshine" to complete C.J.'s ensemble, Nina often joked.

"Hey, why don't you use the key I gave you?" C.J. asked as Nina stepped inside.

The sisters shared a long, warm embrace. "'Cause I don't want to come bustin' all up in here in case you're . . . um . . . entertaining, if you catch my drift." Nina winked, then moved to the sofa to sit.

"Let me worry about that. It's annoying, the way you lay on the damn doorbell. Use your key next time. That's why I gave it to you in the first place."

C.J. padded across the carpeted floor in her bare feet, then plopped on the sofa beside her sister.

"So, you won't have company tonight? What happened to Eric?"

"Had to kick that one to the curb," C.J. revealed nonchalantly. "He started getting too clingy. And wanting more of my time than I could give him."

"Oh c'mon, C.J. Eric seemed like a nice enough guy, and he was loaded, wasn't he?"

"He was OK and he was fun . . . *at first*. But then he had to go ruin things by getting weird on me. *Da-dup da-dup da-dup da-dup*," C.J. performed her version of the *Twilight Zone* theme music. "Started acting kinda stalkerish and all."

"Stalkerish? How in the world was he stalking you? Telepathically?" Nina laughed. "You're not in town long enough, always on the go, go, go."

"Eric lives way across town and wouldn't know his dipstick from a swizzle stick, so what was he doing in *my* neighborhood AutoZone store for the third time in one week? When I just happened to be there shopping? And when he passed, like, two closer AutoZones en route?"

Nina shrugged. "I don't know. Maybe he just happened to be taking care of some other business this way and decided he was in dire need of spare auto parts and supplies."

"Right," C.J. deadpanned. "Three times? He just happened to need auto parts when he just happened to be in my neighborhood? And besides, he can't even drive wheels with a manual transmission."

"Imagine that!" Nina gasped with sarcasm, slapping her hands against her cheeks.

C.J. crinkled her nose. "You know, I've always thought there was something a little off about a man who can't drive a stick."

Nina shook her head. "You're crazy and nitpicking *again*. You're too hard on a decent prospect just when the goin' gets good."

"What-ev-er," C.J. grumbled. "Believe me, it was time to give ol' Eric the boot. And he was just a bit too obsessed with fondue and tapas restaurants to suit my taste."

"Hey, I love tapas restaurants!" Nina patted her toned tummy. "Those itty-bitty servings are perfect for my diet."

"I prefer meat-and-potatoes men with hearty appetites."

Nina shook her head. "If those are all of Eric's flaws, it's a short list."

"He knew all the lyrics to the latest Broadway show tunes. I could go on," C.J. warned, then burst out in chuckles along with Nina.

"Seriously, C.J., are you ever going to settle down? Your short-and-sweets, as you call them, must be getting pretty old right about now."

"I suggest you pay attention to getting your own love life in order. You're still single, too, or hadn't you noticed?"

"But I want to get married and I'm actively

searching for Mr. Right. I just haven't found him yet."
Nina had always been the die-hard romantic and op-
timist of the two.

The harsh realities of life had made C.J. way
more pragmatic. "Well, um, I haven't found him yet,
either."

"And you've been looking?" Nina asked, looking
doubtful. "We'll both be thirty in three years. We're
burning off good childbearing years, ya know. I'm
more than ready for my prince to come."

"You've been reading way too many romance
novels, girl." C.J. made a face.

"It couldn't hurt you to read a few. Could learn a
thing or two to help you lighten up and be more positive about the future."

When C.J. had been sick, bored, and bedridden for
the umpteenth time she had read a few of Nina's stu-
pid novels. However, on those pages she never found
a brassy, style-challenged, gear-headed hypochondriac, who was capable of entertaining herself with
the right sex toys, a pack of C batteries, and *Playgirl*
magazines. In other words, women such as C.J. did
not get the fairy-tale ending. They did not waltz off
with the men of their dreams.

"You know how much I love my job, but it makes
anything beyond my short-and-sweets way too challenging right now. What can I say?" C.J. shrugged.
"Most men looking for something serious are put
off by what I do."

"And, Sis, I do wonder if you chose that work for

that very reason, so you could tell yourself you can't open your heart to someone."

C.J. took a long reflective moment. "What can I say? I'm just a road warrior–trucker chick, who prefers to travel light."

Many people just didn't get it. Why on earth would any woman actually want this sort of life?

When most teenage girls were preparing to head off to college, C.J. had been sick, hospital- or bed-bound, so it felt as if she'd been playing catch-up ever since. She had an overwhelming desire for freedom. Over the past seven years she'd already visited forty-one states. Few jobs could compare with hers for satisfying that yen to see the country as well as providing a decent salary, lots of vacation, and flexible hours if needed.

"You and I both know what's going on here, C.J. You can't fool me and I know you're not as happy with the status quo as you pretend to be. You should at least *try* to exorcise your demons instead of running away from them."

With that, C.J. came to her feet to end this subject. "I need a drink. Can I get you something?"

"A beer would be nice," Nina said, obviously choosing not to hassle C.J. further about her lifestyle. While Nina was set on what she wanted out of life—a husband and a houseful of kids—she still had her own issues and was hardly in a position to judge C.J.'s choices.

There had never been a shortage of men interested

in Nina and C.J., because of their good looks. But with C.J., guys rarely got beyond three or four dates. Maybe—if they were *really* lucky and the mood struck her—there would be a few hot nights, too. Men had been temporary indulgences for her. They were merely used to relieve stress, much like a good foot massage or pint of Ben & Jerry's Chubby Hubby ice cream.

Her restless spirit and chronic wanderlust made bonding, beyond the superficial, too difficult. Building and nurturing something more substantial and long-term required way more stability than C.J. could muster. She'd spent the last few years on the road. Her home away from home: the nation's highways and the semitruck she used for work—a Volvo 660 with its 430/500 Detroit Diesel engine that had 679,000 miles on it. The engine was already past its warranty, but she saw no reason that she wouldn't get a million more miles out of it with a good maintenance program. And that's exactly what she planned to do—if time allowed. The ticking of the clock was the sound track for her life. And she couldn't move beyond that feeling that she was running out of time.

C.J. went to the kitchen. When she returned to the living room with two beers, Nina had made herself more comfortable and removed the platform sandals from her own feet.

C.J. passed one of the chilled bottles to Nina. "Oh, guess what I found today!" C.J.'s voice hitched an octave with enthusiasm as she dropped on the sofa again. She couldn't believe it hadn't spilled out of her as soon as Nina stepped inside her house. "You know I've been looking for just the right one for a while now. And I finally found it."

Mirroring her sister, Nina's face brightened and her body snapped to attention. "What? What?"

"Get this! I found a Barracuda!" C.J. squealed, resting her bottle on the coffee table to flap her arms wildly.

"*The* Barracuda, right?" Nina sipped her beer.

"Yup. Got it from this north-side woman who inherited it after her father passed away."

"That's great, C.J.!" Nina said, though C.J. realized her sister wasn't nearly as excited as she pretended to be. If it wasn't a brand spanking new European ride with a sexy male driver behind the wheel, Nina couldn't care less about cars.

C.J., on the other hand, was a die-hard grease monkey. She had always been a sucker for all cars and trucks. Photos and minireplicas of various makes and models of vehicles still decorated the walls and shelves of her home. As teens, Nina flipped through stacks of *Vogue, Glamour,* and *Essence,* while C.J. absorbed everything in *Car and Driver, Hot Rod,* and *Motor Trend.*

"Tell me more," Nina managed anyway with a polite smile.

"Well, it's a 1971 Plymouth Barracuda, a real-deal muscle car," C.J. gushed. "Know what this means, don't you?"

Nina nodded. "You'll participate in this year's Woodward Dream Cruise—*finally*! I'm so excited for you!"

C.J. let loose with another squeal and pumped her fist. "Yes!"

The decade-old event that had C.J. so hyped up had become a unique tradition in the Motor City. Each year auto enthusiasts from all over the world flocked to the city to participate in the caravan or vie for prime seats, curbside lawn chairs that stretched along the Dream Cruise route. Tens of thousands of classic cars of every ilk rolled up the stretch of Woodward Avenue from Ferndale to Pontiac. Last year's event attracted approximately 2 million people.

C.J. had dreamed about participating in the annual event since they were teens.

"So this car, though it's a 1971 model, is in pristine shape and ready to go?" Nina asked, then took a sip of her beer.

"Well, not exactly."

"It needs a little work? More than the tinkering that's your specialty?"

"I'm afraid so. It needs a brand-new engine, but it also needs a ton of bodywork. The outside is pretty banged up and rusted. The panels and frame rails are wrecks, and the trunk's bottom is nonexistent."

"Sounds like a heap, a real hoopty, if you ask me."

"It's not a hoopty!" C.J. scowled.

"Outside pumping gas and tracking my tune-ups and oil changes, I'll admit I don't know diddly about cars, but is that thing even salvageable? It sounds as if it needs a lot of work *and* cash to me. Think you can really get it all done in time for the Dream Cruise? Isn't that just a few weeks away?"

"Six weeks to be exact, but where there's a will . . ."

"Where is this car, by the way? In your garage?"

"It's still at the seller's place."

"And why is that?"

"I'll have to arrange to have a tow truck pick it up," C.J. said sheepishly. "And it's perched on cement blocks right now."

"Cement blocks? The thing is not even drivable!" Nina twisted her lips in disapproval. "C.J.!"

"It's a *classic ride.*" C.J. lifted her chin defiantly. "And it's gonna be a sweet one, too, once it gets the TLC it needs. Just wait and see."

"For you and your bank account's sake I hope you're right."

"I've been putting money aside for a while now especially for this project," C.J. said.

Nina paused thoughtfully. "I know this is something you've wanted for a long time, so I won't pee on your parade anymore. Sorry if I didn't sound very optimistic. I just hope you didn't buy yourself a total lemon that'll morph into one big headache for you."

"It won't. I just have a feeling . . ."

"You know your cars. Go for it. Whatever you need me to do to help make it happen, just let me know."

C.J. drew in Nina for a hug, then pressed a kiss of gratitude on her soft cheek. "Thanks for your support, Sis. And of course, you have the honor of taking the coveted passenger's seat if you want it. I can see it now." She lifted one hand in the air as if gesturing toward a big cineplex screen that played her dream of how it would unfold. "The Davis twins stylin' and profilin' down Woodward Avenue in my spiffed-up 'Cuda! Can you see it? It's going to be great!"

C.J. knew tooling down Woodward in a resuscitated muscle car was far from Nina's idea of an exciting summer night on the town, but loved her for not bursting her sister's bubble by admitting it at that moment.

C.J. broke into an off-key rendition of an ol' Smokey Robinson song: "I looooove it when we're cruis-in' to-ge-ther!" She slapped Nina on the back, encouraging her to sing along.

Then C.J. came to her feet. She tugged Nina off the sofa to sweep her across the floor for an impromptu waltz as they sang.

Laughing, Nina fell in step, getting caught up in C.J.'s infectious glee.

3

Ethan Tanner placed a bundle of daisies near the headstone of one grave, then arranged a dozen Beanie Babies around the small headstone next to it.

He said a prayer for two souls he tried convincing himself were now in a better place. Still, the pain of the tragic loss made his chest heavy and his chin tremble. The images appeared crisp and clear: A vibrant young woman who lived to laugh, play piano, design jewelry, and tend to her rose garden surfaced. The most adorable chubby-cheeked girl in a pink leotard and tutu performing an awkward pirouette on a makeshift set with handmade props fashioned from foil and tissue paper. Sounds of mingled laughter—mother and daughter—as they baked saucer-sized chocolate-chip cookies and made a mess in a sunny Farmington Hills kitchen.

Familiar sorrow weighed down Ethan's bones; then a warm hand encircled his forearm, startling him out of his reverie. He turned to see Beatrice Whitmore at his side. The usual sparkle in her brown eyes was muted, but a small, comforting smile curved her lips. Though attractive, she appeared older than her fifty-five years. Losing a beloved daughter and granddaughter could do that.

"Hello, Ethan, dear," Beatrice said softly, releasing the arm to clasp his hand for emotional support.

Ethan bent his tall frame to plant a kiss on her powdered and perfumed cheek. "Hello, Beatrice. So good to see you."

It was then Ethan noticed Beatrice wasn't alone. Her husband, Stan, and a close family friend, Jacinda Hughes, hovered near.

Ethan wondered if they'd just arrived or if they'd opted to stand by to allow Ethan his private time with memories of the wife and child he had lost in a car crash a year and a half ago.

"Hello, Jacinda." Ethan moved to kiss her cheek, then faced the man at her side. "Stan," Ethan acknowledged his former father-in-law with a respectful nod. It was obvious from the hard set of Stan's blocklike jaw and the iced look in his dark brown eyes that the older man's attitude toward Ethan had not changed with time.

Ethan suspected Stan was grateful for the

voluminous bouquets he carried so he had an excuse not to shake Ethan's hand. Stan held more daisies, Leigh-Ann's favorite flowers, and stuffed teddy bears to decorate Hailey's grave site.

Only after Beatrice cut Stan a warning glare did the older man respond. With an uncomfortable expression on her face, Jacinda quietly took it all in.

"Ethan," Stan managed the curt greeting as his stocky frame went stiff from the effort.

"It's still hard to believe they're gone." With her free hand Beatrice dabbed at her eyes with a wadded tissue. "Well, not really gone. Leigh-Ann and Hailey will always live in our hearts."

Jacinda cut in as tears slipped down her cheeks. "As long as we love and cherish their memories they'll always be with all of us."

Jacinda and Beatrice squeezed Ethan's hands again.

"It's important that we honor Leigh-Ann's wishes," Beatrice said. "She wouldn't want us spatting. You two did enough of that when she was alive." She shot her husband another irritated look. "The least we all can do is let her rest in peace. It would've been her thirty-first birthday today."

Stan cleared his throat, then surprised Ethan by inquiring about his mental and physical states as if he actually cared.

"There are good days and bad days. And you?"

"Same here," Stan replied.

The sun suddenly slipped behind a thick blanket

of clouds. Startling brightness soon gave way to a moody gray. "Looks as if we might get some rain today after all," Beatrice said.

With a grimace, Ethan looked up at the sky, which reflected his overall disposition. "Yeah, sure it does."

"If you don't have plans, join us later, dear. Stan and I would love to have you over for dinner. Jacinda's coming," Beatrice said. "It would also give us a chance to talk about the upcoming gala for the scholarship fund."

Beatrice and Jacinda might have wanted his company that evening, but despite his former father-in-law's temporary cease-fire, Ethan realized he was the last person Stanley Whitmore would want to spend time with on his deceased daughter's birthday. Not when Ethan was sure Stan still held him at least partially responsible for what happened that tragic winter night when the car Leigh-Ann was driving had slid and spun along an ice-plated road, then collided with an oncoming vehicle, killing Leigh-Ann, Hailey, and the other driver instantly. Stan had yet to forgive Ethan for what happened that night. He knew how much Leigh-Ann dreaded driving in treacherous winter weather. She'd attempted to conquer that fear that night to get an ailing Hailey, who was running a high temperature, to an emergency room anyway. Ethan was supposed to be home with his family that night but got delayed at the shop for something that was so insignificant, in hindsight he couldn't even recall what it was. All he knew was that at the time he'd been putting in more and more long hours to ensure the chain of auto repair and body shops he owned remained a success. Frantic, Leigh-Ann had phoned him at his office that night to tell him she was worried about Hailey, and he'd advised his wife to sit tight. He hadn't thought an ambulance was necessary. He was soon on his way home to drive them to the hospital. He'd raced as fast as he could on dangerously slick streets as he endured low, snow-blurred visibility. By the time he'd arrived at their Farmington Hills home, however, Leigh-Ann had already left, choosing to navigate glasslike highways. Ethan couldn't help thinking if he'd been there that tragedy could've been avoided.

"Sorry, I've got plans. Rain check?" Ethan wrapped an arm around Beatrice's shoulder and placed a quick kiss on her forehead. "But I would like us all to get together. Real soon. I'll give you a call early next week so we can set up something."

"That sounds good. You know I still think of you as part of our family, dear, just like Jacinda is still a part of us," Beatrice said just before a light misting rain started falling. She removed her lightweight suit jacket to shield her coif of feathery curls.

Stan placed the bouquets and stuffed animals on the two graves. He, Beatrice, and Jacinda said quick prayers before dashing off along the lush manicured grass toward their black Buick. Ethan assumed the trio would depart, but they obviously planned to wait out the rain or wait out Ethan, then return to Leigh-Ann's and Hailey's grave sites.

Ethan didn't mind the rain so much. He let it soak into his usual work attire—an oxford shirt, lightweight cotton jacket, and khaki slacks. The light, warm mist eventually gave way to cool, hard drops that pelted his face. While he had been submerged and drowned in grief, it was if he was struggling to catch his breath for months after he lost his wife and daughter. Though he still missed them, something inside had begun to unclench three months ago. He'd felt Leigh-Ann's presence. He was sure it was brought on by the vivid dream he'd had about her. It was as if she stood beside his bed. She looked so real, he could reach out and touch her. Her smile was as beautiful and compassionate as he'd remembered. She'd whispered, "We know you loved us and a part of you always will, but it's time. Seek some new joy."

His heart still had an achy, hollow spot that felt as deep as the Grand Canyon some days, but he awoke the morning after that dream with something he hadn't felt in a while: hope. He could finally take a deep breath. He could and would move on.

4

It had been a week and two days since C.J. purchased the Barracuda. Soon it would be fully restored to its former beauty. The thought gave her the best kind of chills.

With an ink pen clenched between her teeth she hunched over the desk in her home office skimming the short list of auto repair and body shops she'd visited to discuss the needed repairs. They weren't up for the job, in her opinion. Only the best for her baby. She'd done her research and there was only one team she was willing to trust, but it had to be fast. She only had five more weeks until the Dream Cruise. She had settled back in her chair, picturing herself in the car, when she noticed that the pesky little twitch again. Familiar fear skimmed up her spine. "What the hell . . . ?" It had bothered her since she'd made that run to Texas four weeks ago, and had grown stronger, moving from a front thigh muscle up an arm to her hand.

The fleshy area just below her thumb pulsed for a few seconds before it stilled again. C.J.'s mouth went dry and her heart thumped inside her chest. "It's probably nothing," she said out loud. "Don't start freakin' the hell out again."

Drawing deep, calming breaths seemed to do the trick, but she knew that wouldn't work for long.

She wouldn't relax until she paid a visit to Kaye. So what if it was her fifth visit to a physician in the past three months? Kaye didn't know that. Three of those visits had been to those quickie in-and-out clinics C.J. had found while on the road. She hadn't even bothered to present her insurance card for the bill, instead charging the visits to her Visa.

She reached for the phone and dialed Kaye's family medicine practice. They could fit her in that day's schedule if she could get there within an hour. C.J., who'd zipped through two yellow lights, made it there in seventeen minutes. She sat, legs dangling from the table in the examining room, as Dr. Kaye Anderson, a middle-aged woman with graying dreadlocks and hazel eyes, took her through the paces with the tongue compressor and stethoscope. Kaye had been the Davis family doctor for several years and had also become a trusted family friend. Kaye was the only one who knew that tough, trash-talking

C.J. always sweated the small stuff when it came to her health.

"So how long have you been noticing these twitches, C.J.?" Kaye asked, shining a beam of white laserlike light inside C.J.'s left ear.

"A few weeks now, about four weeks."

"And they come and go?"

"Yeah, but I've noticed that when they return they get stronger than the time before. I've been doing some reading on the Internet. Went to some chat rooms, medical forums, and message boards—"

"And scared the living daylights out of yourself as usual, I'm sure." Kaye gave C.J. a reprimanding look and planted one hand on an ample hip. "Thought I told you to stay away from those darn Internet boards."

"But I'm learning things. It's not all bad."

"Of course there is some good medical information out there on the Web, but you have to be careful. A lot of it is not only inaccurate but potentially dangerous—especially when people start taking the advice as gospel. Advice coming from anonymous sources with no medical training."

"But—"

"OK, out with it. So what is it that you think you might have now?"

"Well." C.J. swallowed, then wrung her hands. "I did a search on recurring muscle twitches and it seems they can be a symptom of MS or ALS." C.J. looked Kaye in the eye as goose bumps prickled her skin.

"Multiple sclerosis *and* Lou Gehrig's disease? Hmmm, now those are new ones for you." Kaye kept the judgment out of her tone, though she must have thought C.J. was more than a few sandwiches shy of a full picnic by now. The most annoying kind of hypochondriac to have as a patient. The type who did her research, made up her mind enough to self-diagnose, then only approached a doctor to confirm.

Kaye extended her hands. "Push down as hard as you can against my palms."

C.J. did as instructed for the next ten minutes while Kaye led her through a series of moves to test her reflexes and muscle strength in all of her limbs. The exam ended after Kaye rattled off an extensive list of questions attached to her clipboard.

When Kaye was all done she pushed out a sigh, then shrugged. "I'm not sure what to tell you, C.J. But from what I can tell, everything's checking out fine. I'm noticing no muscle wasting or weakness."

C.J. threw up her hands. "But I'm not imagining these freakin' twitches, just as I didn't imagine that those two flat brown spots on my chest a few months ago had grown larger than the head of a pencil eraser."

"And I referred you to a specialist, a dermatologist, remember?"

"Yes."

"And if I'm not mistaken, based on the report he sent along with his test results and his diagnosis, it wasn't melanoma as you'd assumed. They weren't even moles but spots of seborrheic keratoses, benign brown growths." Kaye then added, "They're commonly referred to as barnacles of old age, you know."

"Barnacles of old age?" C.J. screeched. "But I'm only twenty-seven, for crying out loud!"

Kaye chuckled lightly. "Apparently young people aren't immune to them. We don't know why they appear exactly, but the general consensus is that they're harmless." Kaye scribbled something on a notepad. "I think you're fine, as you've been for a while now, C.J." Kaye sobered a bit and placed a comforting hand on C.J.'s arm. "But I do understand your fears, after everything you've been through."

"Thanks," C.J. said solemnly as she slipped off the examining table. She moved toward the street clothes neatly stacked on a chair and removed the light blue hospital gown she'd donned for the exam.

"Because I know it'll make you feel better I'm going to go ahead and give you a referral to a good neurologist so he can check out those annoying muscle twitches you've been experiencing. But stand warned, he'll probably want to give you an EMG, which involves poking several needles into your muscles to test electrical activity."

A few needles? Bring 'em on! C.J. had endured worse—much worse—starting three weeks before her and Nina's fifteenth birthday bash.

It was when C.J. had discovered the suspicious lump under her right arm while in the shower. The diagnosis: Hodgkin's disease. Cancer of the lymphatic system, which carried white blood cells that fought infection, to be exact. For the next two and a half years she'd endured high doses of chemo and radiation as well as countless tests, scans, and visits to oncology specialists.

C.J.'s illness had not only turned her young life upside down; it had also affected the rest of the Davises and skewed their family dynamics in both positive and negative ways. C.J. had never felt so loved and close to her parents, her twin, and Aunt Ella. But at the same time, C.J. sensed that her disease had sucked a whole lot of normalcy out of their home lives with all the focus centered on her most of the time. Even after she'd completed that first series of treatments and been told she was cancer-free, things had never been the same as they were before that first diagnosis. She still felt overly coddled. And *handled*. It was as if her parents thought she'd shatter if they ever said or did anything to rattle her in the least. It was a wonder she hadn't gone into a diabetic coma from all the sugarcoating they did where C.J. was concerned. Her corny jokes were the funniest they'd ever heard. Instead of chalking up her no-fuss approach to her appearance to laziness, they thought it gave her a depth her more flighty fashion-conscious twin lacked. And where C.J.'s job was concerned, they'd never verbally expressed disapproval, but she'd recognized the fleeting looks of disappointment and sheer terror in their eyes when she first told them she planned to take to the nation's highways—all alone—in a big rig. "Whatever makes you happy, C.J., we're all behind you," was all her parents had said.

Bottom line: C. J. Davis could say or do no wrong as far as her parents were concerned. And it was a wonder Nina hadn't turned on her because of it.

Thank God for Nina and their aunt Ella. C.J. could still count on those two to be straight with her.

C.J. realized, however, that her parents weren't the only ones with issues. She still had enough of her own emotional baggage to fill the bowels of a jumbo jet.

In the back of her mind there was always that persistent fear of recurrence, which was heightened by the fact that she had endured a second attack by cancer. At age nineteen, she'd sought treatment for a stubborn eye infection and it was discovered that she had AML, acute myeloid leukemia, a type of cancer of the blood that required even more aggressive treatment in the form of a bone marrow transplant, which she got from Nina. Fortunately, the procedure had been successful.

At age twenty-seven C.J. had been cancer-free for almost seven full years, but the slightest ailment or symptom out of the ordinary—an eye twitch, stubborn ache, mysterious bump, spot of rash, tiny bruise, or skin discoloration—often sent her hightailing it to a doctor's office before one could utter "HMO."

Some days she thought the extreme paranoia—where her health was concerned—that stalked her every move like a shadow would drive her nuts. No matter how energetic she felt or how glowing she looked, she simply could not get past the feeling that she was doomed to meet her maker at a young age.

5

Inside the Southfield office attached to Ethan's flagship auto repair shop, he'd immersed himself in the usual day-to-day business of running his chain. His mouth was dry when he decided a cold soft drink from the fridge in the staff's break room was just the reprieve he'd earned, but not before checking on some of the vehicles entrusted to his company's care.

Ethan stepped out of his air-conditioned space into the garage's warmer service bays area, where the usual scents of motor oil and gasoline hung in the air. He consulted with Gary, the mechanic who had a Porsche hoisted on a lift, until he caught a glimpse of a young woman climbing out of a gray pickup out front. She looked familiar. The longer he stared, the more sure he was that he knew her. But how? Through the open garage door his gaze followed her to the glass-encased reception area. Most of the men in the shop who weren't working and a few who were supposed to be working admired her looks—the angelic face and the sinfully sexy figure. The woman was a knockout even in a faded black T-shirt and no-frills blue jeans. A lustrous ponytail spilled out the back of the Tigers baseball cap on her head.

"The owner wants this back by late tomorrow. Not sure we can promise that." Gary proceeded to rattle off a string of details about the Porsche.

"Have you told him that already?" Ethan was still staring at the woman.

Gary noticed and cleared his throat in a not-so-subtle effort to get his boss's full attention. "Yeah, but he's insisting."

Ethan blinked and faced Gary again.

"There's no way we can get the new parts in by then and give it the kind of attention a job like this would require." Gary wiped his hands on a rag, then tucked it back in the pocket of his grease-stained overalls.

"Well, if he won't listen to reason he'll have to take his business elsewhere." Again Ethan looked beyond his employee to search for the woman in the baseball cap. He slapped Gary on the back to signal that he was moving on, then strolled to the reception area.

Sid, the shop's manager, and the woman didn't

notice as Ethan made a show of rifling through the tall file cabinets lined there. He wasn't searching for anything in particular. He just wanted to get a closer look at the woman and eavesdrop to satisfy his curiosity. His actions befuddled him. This wasn't his style and he'd never shown such intense personal interest in any customer before. *Where had he seen her before?*

The woman spoke to Sid, who listened quietly as he scribbled notes on a clipboard. She told him the reason for her visit. And it had nothing to do with the shiny late-model Dodge pickup she'd arrived in. Much to Ethan's pleasant surprise, she was gushing over an old Barracuda. That's when it hit him. It was the pushy woman who had poached his 'Cuda a week ago and pissed him the hell off! He'd simmered about that incident for two whole days. He'd been seconds from closing the deal with Kathy when the chick in a baseball cap not only interrupted their transaction but also blew him out of the water. OK, so he'd *let* her blow him out of the water. He had more than enough cash in the bank to hang with her in a bidding war, but he chose not to. He'd sensed desperation in her, so he'd backed down. He told himself there'd be other Barracudas. But that did not completely take the edge off his loss.

Ethan continued to study her from his spot near the file cabinets. *What was her name?*

She displayed a brilliant smile and her hands moved with quick, animated gestures as she spoke.

Odd. He knew it was sexist and narrow-minded, but he'd didn't think many women her age would be all that interested in an old muscle car that probably rolled off the assembly line before she was born and long before she was old enough to drive. She could not have cracked thirty yet. There was something about her body language and that gorgeous honey-colored skin that glowed with twenty-something vigor.

"Of course, we'll need to take a look at it first before we can promise anything," Sid said as he perused his notes, then shook his head. "But based on what you've told me it needs, I'm pretty sure we can't get it done in time. I mean, getting some of the necessary parts in will take a while. This is a lot of work, lady. And we already have a full load."

"But you're the best in town," she said. "I've done my homework. Your reputation—"

"Yes, we're good at what we do, but we don't rush jobs," Sid said. "Sorry, we can't help you. We'd have to arrange for some of our best men to work overtime. I certainly don't have the authority to approve such a move. The owner would have to green-light it."

Though frustrated, she appeared far from defeated. "But there *must* be something you can do," she pleaded, and tried a more personal approach as she picked out the shop manager's name on the tag stitched to his jumpsuit. "Sid, work with me here. It would mean so much to me."

"Well, um . . ." Sid wavered a bit—a pretty face could do that to the strongest of men—but he remained steadfast. "You'll have to talk to the owner."

Ethan took that as his cue to butt in, so he strolled over, hands shoved deep in his pants pockets. "Excuse me."

She turned around.

The instant she saw him a hint of recognition sparked in her eyes. "Hey, don't I know you?"

"Allow me to introduce myself. I'm Ethan, the guy whose 'Cuda you stole," he said in a smart-ass manner as he removed one hand from his pocket and extended it.

The woman furrowed her brow and refused to shake his hand. "I did not, I repeat, did not steal *your* 'Cuda. From what I understand there was no official deal, because no papers had been signed."

"A technicality. Kathy and I had a verbal agreement, that is, until you horned in." Ethan found it hard to maintain his confrontational tone when he had the pleasure of standing so close to her. She was even prettier than he remembered. And she had the most mesmerizing eyes. Huge. Coffee brown. Full of fire.

"Hey, Kathy broke a promise to you; I didn't," she pointed out matter-of-factly before bunching up those luscious lips of hers.

"No, you just jacked up a business deal in the works," Ethan said.

"Right. You hit the nail right on the head. *Business*. It was just business, nothing personal."

"You don't say?" Ethan replied with more than a hint of sarcasm as he egged her on.

She clucked her tongue. "Look, you lost out. Get over it." She inched closer to clap him on the back. "Be a man about it, all right?"

Ethan's eyebrows hitched high. She was obnoxious and condescending to boot. But hell, he kinda liked her.

She went on, "I know it must be hard to accept. But I'm not going to stand here and blow smoke up your butt—and pretend that I'm sorry I got the car, because we both know that would be a load of bull."

"Well, thank you for not insulting my intelligence." Ethan's demeanor was reserved, but he really wanted to smile.

"Maybe if I explained." Her voice sounded warmer and her expression relaxed this time. "You see, I've been looking for a car exactly like that one for ages; then when I finally found it, well, the adrenaline just kicked in. And I was hell-bent on doing whatever it took to make it mine."

"I understand now," Ethan replied evenly with a slow nod.

His response obviously brought her up short. "You do? No hard feelings, then?"

"None. Bygones."

"Good," she replied. "Now, if you could just take a seat over there, I'll finish my business with Sid here; then you get your turn." Then as if dangling a treat too tantalizing to pass up, she added, "Hey, I think I noticed that they have the latest issue of *Custom & Collector Car* magazine on the coffee table over there, Evan."

"It's *Ethan*," he said.

"You might get lucky and find another '71 'Cuda. Maybe one that's in better shape than mine." She gave him a quick smile.

"It's worth a shot, I guess." Ethan decided to play along.

Sid gave Ethan a befuddled look before Ethan strolled off, whistling all the way to the lounge area.

"Now where were we?" Ethan heard the woman ask Sid before he was out of earshot.

Ethan took a seat in a chair near the soft drink machine, then did as she suggested and lifted the issue of *Custom & Collector Car* magazine off the coffee table. He made himself comfortable, settling back in the seat, lifting his right ankle to rest on his left knee. He flipped through the pages, then looked across the room and watched her continue her conversation with Sid. Ethan checked the second hand on his wristwatch and began his countdown. *Ten, nine, eight, seven, six—*

The next thing Ethan knew, he sensed her presence and savored her fragrance. Whatever she was wearing, it wasn't from a fancy bottle. It was cleaner. He guessed it was her natural scent mingled with soap.

Though she stood before him, he kept his head bowed, nose in the magazine. In his peripheral vision he noted the clunky Doc Marten–style black boots on her feet. She cleared her throat to get his attention.

"Finish your business with Sid already?" he asked cheerfully as he pretended to be too engrossed in an article on Chevy Chevelles to look up.

"Why didn't you tell me you were the owner of Tanner's, *Ethan Tanner*?" she wanted to know.

"You were so busy shooing me away as if I were some mangy flea-bitten stray, you didn't give me or Sid a chance."

"Sorry about that," she offered. "I was so eager to get on with business."

He still wouldn't look up.

"You're not making a very good first or second impression, lady," he said coolly, then flipped a page.

"I know." She sighed, shifting her weight from one clunky boot to the other. "About that day at Kathy's, I was . . . um . . . just so focused on . . . um . . . my own interest—"

"The word is '*selfish*,' " he cut in, casually flipping another page, still refusing to give her his undivided attention. "Go on."

"OK, I was selfish and today I've been . . . um . . ."

"I believe the word is '*rude*', extremely rude. Go on." He flipped yet another page.

"I've been selfish and rude. And after all that, I need to ask you for a *huge* favor."

"Figures."

"A really huge favor, actually."

"Oh, but I do like the way you don't beat around the bush. You cut straight to the chase."

"Right, so here's the deal . . ."

Ethan finally closed the magazine and gave her his full attention. He anchored both feet on the floor, placed the magazine on the end table, then sat back again, crossing his arms across his broad chest. "What is it? Shoot."

"About the Barracuda that I practically stole from you . . . ," she began.

She tried to sound sincere, but Ethan knew she was just playing him.

"By the way, has anyone ever told you that you could pass for Taye Diggs's taller, finer, buffer brother?" she added, scorching him with an appraising look from head to toe.

Ethan replied, eyes unblinking, "I take back what I said about your cutting to the chase and not beating around the bush." He tsk-tsked her. "Now I'm disappointed. I mean, I was sorta impressed, in a peculiar sort of way, until you resorted to cheesy compliments that seem beneath a no-nonsense spitfire such as yourself."

"Oh, but you *are* gorgeous as all get-out," she said, batting her lashes and trying on a guileless expression that didn't fit. "Thought I'd cut to the chase and let you know that I do find you very attractive."

Ethan would've enjoyed the flattery and returned

it wholeheartedly had she not already proven she'd do or say anything when it came to that old 'Cuda. "Well, thank you. Now about your car . . ."

"It needs a lot of body- and under-hood work, as I'm sure you already know because you checked it out before making Kathy an offer."

"Yes, I did. And we do just the kind of work it needs right here. We're the best in town for the money, so you came to the right place."

"The thing is I need the work done in time for the Dream Cruise in about five weeks. Sid tells me it wouldn't be a problem if you weren't already so booked up—"

"Yup, business is booming," Ethan said, quite pleased that he had the upper hand. "And the tight deadline you're giving us makes your request darn near impossible."

"You said 'darn near impossible,' not 'impossible,' which means there must be a way to make it happen, working it in, I mean, so the car is finished in time."

"I suppose that could happen . . . *if* I wanted it to," Ethan said, taking in how damn alluring she was. Femininity wasn't about wearing frilly clothing, playing coy, or waiting for a big, strong man to take the lead and make the first move. This woman exuded a type of sex appeal that only the most secure of men could appreciate. Her confident take-charge, go-for-it, and screw-you-if-you-don't-like-it manner turned him on.

"And what would it take for you to want to, Mr. Tanner?"

"Hmmm, let me think about that." Ethan rubbed his chin as if in deep thought, though he'd already made up his mind to help the lady out—no strings attached. She'd intrigued the hell out of him.

"I'll pay extra, within reason, of course. I'll even grovel, but only up to a point. I'd really appreciate it if you'd accept my business."

"OK. Deal. Where is the car?"

"So Tanner's will do the work . . . in time for the Dream Cruise?" Her beautiful face brightened with hope.

"Yeah, I'll make sure the job gets worked in . . . at no extra charge."

"Oh, thank you! Thank you!" She beamed and reached for his hand to shake. "You don't know how much I appreciate this—especially after our rocky start."

It made Ethan feel good to see her smile. "Now where's that car?" he asked again, standing to his full six feet, four inches, and beckoning Sid.

"Still on the north side at Kathy's house. As you know, it has to be towed," C.J. said, tipping her head to look up at him.

"We're a full-service shop, so Tanner's will take care of that."

"Sweet!" she said as Sid joined them. "He agreed to take on the car!" she told the manager excitedly.

Ethan could feel Sid's puzzled gaze burning a hole in the side of his head.

"How soon can you have your guys pick it up?" she asked.

"Is today good?" Ethan replied with a smile.

"Hell, yeah!" she said quickly.

"Good." Ethan turned to Sid. "Get Monty out there as soon as he returns from his supplies run."

"Yes, sir," Sid said accommodatingly just as Laverne, Ethan's assistant, paged him to take a phone call on line two. He didn't budge. Barracuda Woman had knocked him off his feet, but he still attempted to maintain an air of professionalism. He'd already glanced at her ring finger and found it bare. She did say she found him attractive, but he knew she was just flattering him to get what she wanted. But even if she were genuine, it didn't mean she was available or even remotely interested in actually dating him— especially now that they were going to do business together. It was worth a shot, however. All she could do was turn him down. So? Now that he was open to dating again, rejection would come with the territory. "So we have a plan. What was your name again?"

She placed her hand in his. "C. J. Davis," she said with a firm grip.

"C.J.?" he echoed, curious why she preferred the initials to whatever they stood for.

"C.J."

Ethan held on to her hand. "So is your husband

interested in old muscle cars, too?" he blurted. Uncool. Unsmooth. He might as well have trotted out some tired line asking if she was open, single, and free to mingle.

"Not hitched. And you?" she volleyed, letting him know that his interest and awkward forwardness had not offended her.

In fact, her demeanor remained quite flirtatious. She hadn't withdrawn her hand yet and he wasn't eager to let her go. He'd already agreed to fix her car, so this wasn't about offering herself up for a big favor anymore. Things were getting even more interesting.

"Um, single," he said.

Sid stood there, wide-eyed, as he took in their exchange, but it was obvious neither of them gave a damn.

Ethan and C.J. were clearly checking each other out and liking what they saw until Laverne's voice blared over the intercom again, "Ethan, call for you on line two."

"Better get that," Ethan said, finally releasing C.J.'s hand. "Excuse me." As he moved to take the extension behind the desk at the reception area, he cast glances at C. J. Davis while she boldly eyed Ethan, too. All the while she wore an enticing smile that Ethan returned. Sid jotted down what was most likely the street address where her car was located. A little less than an hour later, when Ethan had finally wrapped up that call from the manager of his

Troy shop, C.J. had departed. Initially disappointed that they couldn't continue their conversation, Ethan took consolation in knowing he would see her again. Soon. That old 'Cuda was a total wreck. But come hell or high water, Tanner's Auto Repair and Body Shop would whip that thing into pristine shape in time for the Dream Cruise.

6

Three days later C.J. didn't awake until late afternoon. She'd greeted that sunny Friday with a helluva hangover from a piña colada overdose the night before. She'd whipped up a batch to celebrate the news she'd received from the neurologist. Dr. Harold Meeks had found no signs of any serious neuromuscular diseases. Like Kaye, he had delivered that info in a *told-you-so* tone.

Even before he'd hooked C.J. up to the EMG machine, he was pretty sure her recurring twitches were no more than something he referred to as "benign, nonpathologic muscle fasciculations," a mouthful that simply translated into harmless muscle spasms that had been exacerbated by the five cans of cola C.J. guzzled each day. She had to lay off the caffeine.

C.J.'s celebration consisted of a party of one. No one in her family—including Nina and Ella—knew about her growing paranoia concerning her health or the recent trips to see various doctors. And she had no close friends in whom to confide.

It wasn't that C.J. didn't like people. She was just extremely cautious about who she let in. She had to be. She'd been devastated when several of her best girlfriends and her junior high school sweetheart had abandoned her at the darkest and scariest points in her life. Just when she'd needed them the most. She realized that even when people had the best of intentions, they often felt too awkward and inadequate when it came to coping with illness. Many believed they never knew what to do or say around those who were withering away right before their eyes. As far as C.J. was concerned, she wasn't looking for deep, philosophical talks or maudlin sentiment worthy of Hallmark about life. Just to have them there would have been more than enough. Instead, one by one, they all became more distant. They had a ton of good excuses why they couldn't visit as often as her illness lingered on. Then one day she looked up and they all had simply vanished.

While in remission, she'd put herself out there again and tried to get on with her life as best she could, but when the cancer returned four years later, the college football player she was dating and her new "friends" also disappeared. While she realized that she'd simply chosen to befriend the wrong type of people, that everyone wouldn't bolt at the first sign of trouble, she simply couldn't muster the fortitude to keep trying or gamble on it happening again. She needed all of her energy to focus on getting well. She wouldn't set herself up for that kind of abandonment and hurt. So except for her family, she couldn't allow herself to get too close to anyone.

She managed to pull herself out of bed to shower and dress. She had to visit Tanner's Auto and Body Shop. A load would take her to Maine in a few days, and she needed to check on the progress the Tanner's team had made on her Barracuda before she took off.

She drove to the auto shop. As she climbed out of her pickup Ethan greeted her.

Her pulse rate zipped. The man was indeed a god, C.J. thought, admiring his strong chiseled features, cleft chin, and wide, cushy mouth. Expansive shoulders and chest filled a light blue pullover shirt, the tail tucked neatly inside crisply pressed navy blue cotton trousers. As far as C.J. was concerned, he had the most perfect male physique she'd ever seen— tall, sleek, and sculpted. Not an ounce of excess fat on his long mocha frame. Probably lived in the gym and ate cleaner than a post-op triple-bypass patient, C.J. suspected.

C.J. waved. "Hi, Ethan."

"Missing your car, huh?" he said, flaunting that dazzling white smile that made her heart go thumpity thump against her chest.

"Yup. I have to go out of town on business for a while. Thought I should check in to see how things are going." C.J. tucked her hands inside the front pockets of her jeans as she trailed Ethan to the service bay where the Barracuda sat.

They paused at the grille of the vehicle.

"All of my guys are good, but Gary, the mechanic I put on this project, is the best of my best," Ethan said. "I told him to give it his complete and undivided attention because this is a very *special* job for a very *special* customer."

"Of course *I* feel that way," she said, "this car is very special, but I'm surprised you feel so strongly about it, too."

"Lady, I intend to make sure you're very happy . . . ," Ethan's voice went low and there was a seductive gleam in his eyes; then he cleared his throat and added, "with Gary's work, I mean."

C.J.'s cheeks warmed under Ethan's unwavering gaze. There was much more behind his remarks, smoldering smile, and hooded eyes than a need to score high ratings for customer service.

"Thank you. I'm sure I will be," C.J. purred as places below her belt sizzled with awareness. What crackled between her and Ethan was off the charts. All she could think at the moment was how much she wanted to rip that shirt from his hot bod to behold what she knew was a strong, broad chest and drum-tight abs underneath. *Later for that,* she said to herself, forcing her attention back to the business at hand. Her car. "May I?" She tapped the hood and Ethan soon had it propped open for her. He leaned one hip against the grille and crossed his arms over his chest.

As C.J. looked inside she could feel Ethan studying her while she used her fingers to poke a grease-stained hose here and prod a worn belt there. She rattled off various auto parts as if the internal workings of a car were a second language for her. She also made astute comments on the work Gary had done so far.

Ethan balanced his weight on both feet again, then took a step inside her personal space. He wasn't touching her, but he seemed to be everywhere and her body exploded with tingles in response. *Hmmp. Hmmp. Hmmp.* They were going to be good, damn good, if they ever got together. His powerful presence and virile magnetism made her dizzy with desire. But she reminded herself to keep her priorities straight. Business now. Fun later if he played his cards right. She took a step away from him to catch her breath and maintained her composure.

Taking a step toward her again, he stole back that space. "Not to come off like a sexist pig or anything, but you're one of only a handful of women I've come across in my life who can peer under a hood and know exactly what they're looking at."

"You don't get around much, do you?" C.J. looked up at him with an indulgent smile. "There are lots of women who can do more than flash a bit of thigh to get help with a flat tire, brotha-man."

"Touché." Ethan grinned, lifting his hands in surrender. "And speaking of tires, as you can see, we put a set of temporary ones on this, just until that flashier set you special-ordered arrive."

C.J. looked away from his face before she got lost in his onyx eyes again, then continued inspecting Gary's handiwork. Most of his effort had been under the hood, but there was still a lot more to be done. The extensive bodywork would come last, when another division of Tanner's took over.

"From what I can tell, everything Gary's done looks decent so far. May I?" C.J. pointed to the clean rag dangling from a nearby hook.

When Ethan nodded his approval she used the rag to wipe the dirt and grease from her hands. "I can't wait to see the finished job."

"Oh, I almost forgot." Ethan tapped the heel of his hand against his forehead. "I hope you don't mind, but I took the liberty of contacting a good friend of mine, who specializes in detecting phony muscle cars, to just make sure that—"

"My Barracuda is not a fake," she finished his sentence matter-of-factly. "And you obviously had a good hunch that it's authentic or you wouldn't have tried to buy it for yourself, right?"

"A good hunch is one thing, but knowing for sure is another," Ethan replied. "Kathy knew the deal would hinge on the results of a thorough inspection.

Can't be too careful. Classic car fraud is big business now. A lot of buyers have been duped into paying big bucks for what they thought were originals only to find out later the cars were merely replicas or clones that should have gone for thousands less than what the buyers paid for them. Why, just eight months ago I had a customer bring in a 1964 GTO he'd purchased at a local car show."

"Whoa, I would've loved to see that one."

"Turns out it was a fake. And I had to give him the bad news."

"Sounds as if he didn't do his homework," C.J. said, looping the rag back on its hook. "I did, but I do appreciate how you went that extra mile to check for me and all. A second opinion is always good. Before I handed over a cashier's check to Kathy I also contacted an expert, who managed to get his hands on factory build sheets for every Plymouth dating back to 1960. He used those and the vehicle identification number to verify the car's authenticity." She added with a proud smile, "This baby is the real deal."

Ethan's admiration for this fascinating woman grew with each encounter. "I should've known you were all over it. You strike me as the take-charge type who leaves nothing to chance. If you have a few minutes I'd love it if you'd join me for a cup of coffee in my office. We could talk cars, muscle cars in particular, and I can show you some pictures of the work we've done on some of the rare models over the years. I have some great digital photos of a Hemi engine–powered Barracuda that was purchased by a customer of mine at an auction. It went for two hundred and fifty thousand dollars and it's the real deal, too."

"Sounds hot," C.J. replied eagerly until she noticed that Ethan was giving her an odd look. "You think I'm very strange, don't you?"

Ethan laughed heartily. "Lady, you have no idea. Truth?"

"Nothing but . . ."

"You're like a breath of fresh air, believe me." What went unsaid was how delectably quirky he found her to be—from her obvious appreciation for hot rods and the growl V-8 engines to her preference for baseball caps, clunky black boots, well-worn T-shirts, and blue jeans. She had thrilled him in a way the overly fastidious and prissy type who had been circling him like vultures since Leigh-Ann died had not.

"So does that 'hot' mean yes, you'll join me in my office for coffee and car talk?"

C.J. paused before answering and he watched her features change from open and lighthearted to closed and subdued in a flash. It was as if she was about to accept his invitation but was waylaid by second thoughts.

"Is something wrong?" Ethan asked, trying to lock gazes with her again.

"Nah." Anxiously, her attention divided between him and the goings-on around the shop. She pasted on a smile that held none of the high-beam spontaneity he had witnessed just minutes before. "Coffee and the classic car photos sound like fun, but I'm afraid I'll have to take a rain check. Maybe another time."

Ethan deflated. "Oh."

"You see, I have a list of things to do a mile long before I take off in a couple of days. I really do need to get my butt in gear."

"You said you had a business trip, right?" Ethan tried to keep the conversation going just a bit longer. He didn't want to let her go.

"Yeah, I'm going to Maine; then I'll head down to D.C."

"And what is it that you do exactly?"

"I do OTR, over-the-road, or long-haul, truck driving."

Ethan went slack-jawed. "You're a . . . a trucker? Meaning you drive an eighteen-wheeler?"

"Actually, the truck itself has ten wheels; I get the other eight when I attach the trailer." C.J. appeared to be studying his reaction.

Ethan had to make sure he came back with the proper response. "Cool," he said, though he was unsure how he really felt about what she'd just revealed.

"Really? You mean that? You think what I do is cool?" Obviously dubious, C.J. lifted a brow.

"Um, y-yeah." He stammered a bit, sounding unconvincing to his own ears.

"Now *that's* a first," she scoffed.

"Hey, you get to see a lot of the country, right?"

C.J. bobbed her head. "Yes, I do. And I love that part."

"You're taller than average, about what? Five-seven?"

"I'm five-eight, one hundred and thirty-two pounds," she replied easily. "What's that got to do with anything?"

Ethan canvassed the delectable curves beneath her jeans and T-shirt. "Looking at your relatively slender build and all, I just never would have guessed."

"It doesn't take bulging muscles or Herculean strength to drive a big rig, honey, but it does require stamina, concentration, and the ability to appreciate your own company for long stretches at a time."

"And you drive alone, too?" Ethan was careful not to judge, though concerns about her safety rose. What kind of life could that possibly be for a young woman? "Wow. You're full of surprises."

"I hope that's a good thing."

He still had so many questions, one of which he wouldn't let go unsaid another moment. "So, when will you return?"

"I'm not sure at this point. Depends on how many stops I'll have to make between Maine and D.C."

"Will you call me when you know?" Ethan reached inside his pocket and removed a business card and pen. He scribbled his cell and home phone numbers on the back. "In case you haven't figured it out by now, I really want to get to know you, lady." He moved closer, then lifted his hand and caressed the silky skin on her cheek with one finger.

C.J.'s lips slowly parted and her tongue darted out to moisten them. A clear invitation for him to move in for a taste of her. He took a step closer, until her breasts grazed his shirt. He wanted to crush her body against his to feel every soft curve meld against the unyielding muscles of his own. It had been so long since he had enjoyed a woman that way, he was hardly surprised by his body's strong, instant yearning for her. She tilted her face up and he dipped his down. Their lips were mere inches apart. But he didn't want their first kiss to happen at his place of business with an audience. Ethan was pretty sure his crew had already taken in way too much of his exchange with C.J. His hands curved around her waist and maneuvered her until her rear met a wall. A towering shelf of auto parts and his frame shielded her from all gawkers, who only had a view of his broad back and boxes lining the shelves. Instead of capturing her mouth with his, he whispered huskily, "Call me," and let his warm breath fan against her cheek. He let one hand move to the flare of her hips. He fought the urge to slip his hand and the card inside the back pocket of her jeans. A brazen move. Stepping way over the line. If it was too soon to get a kiss, it was certainly too soon to cop a feel of her sexy tush.

C.J. looked up at him with glazed eyes, half-mast with just as much desire as he felt.

"Promise me you will call. Soon," he said.

"I will," she murmured through quick breaths.

When she moved closer, he groaned low in his throat. It was then he knew he had to release her and back away.

Though his men couldn't see what was going on, they could guess. He'd let his attraction to C.J. spin out of control, and she deserved better than that sort of public display.

Ethan removed his hand from her hip and took two steps away. And she reacted as if she'd been jolted out of a daze.

The sultry expression on C.J.'s face vanished and she suddenly seemed anxious to retreat. She moved away from the corner and Ethan. "I'd better get going. I've got so much to do to get ready for my trip."

"I know."

"Bye, Ethan," she said, heading out of the service area to her pickup truck out front.

"Wait, I'll walk you." Ethan had to take long strides to catch up to her.

C.J. climbed inside her pickup truck, then closed the driver's side door.

Her silence convinced Ethan that something was wrong. He'd just gotten back in the dating game and his moves were rusty.

She started the engine just as Ethan tapped on the driver's side window. She lowered it.

"I'm sorry if I moved way too fast in there. It's just that . . . Well, it's as if I've been hibernating for over a year and I'm just starting to feel awake again. All these feelings . . . just descended on me at once. Maybe I didn't handle them very well. I hope I didn't offend you. That's usually not my style."

C.J. treated Ethan to a smile, then gave the engine gas. "I'm fine, Ethan. Relax. Everything's cool. Besides, it takes two, ya know." She winked at him. "Anyway, just make sure your guys stay on my car. Talk to you soon." She put the gearshift in reverse.

7

The next day C.J. sat before a bowl of lemons in the Davis family kitchen and watched her mother, Grace, who was a real-life African-American version of a fifties sitcom mom. She still dressed nicely for family dinners—pearls circled her neck and dotted her ears. Her thick brown hair was subdued in a classy French twist and her tiny feet were tucked in navy pumps. She took the time to protect her matching navy sheath dress with a frilly apron. Daintily, she poked at plump golden-brown pieces of chicken sizzling in a cast-iron skillet of grease on the stove.

Grace looked as if she were the type to exist on water with a twist of lemon and finger sandwiches, but she'd actually gotten a lot of use out of that old frying pan, which had been passed down from her great-grandmother. Though well into her fifties, Grace still had the skin and figure that most thirty-somethings would envy. Her time- and gravity-defying good looks weren't due to diet and exercise but stellar genes.

Nina was in charge of chopping vegetables for a big tossed salad.

Malcolm, the patriarch of the Davis family, pushed his burly frame through the swinging door that separated the kitchen from the formal dining room. He had small deep-set eyes, full cheeks that dipped where the deepest dimples flanked his wide smile like parentheses.

He crossed the room to Grace, his wife of thirty years. "I'm all done setting the table, hon." He kissed her cheek and used his thumb to swipe away the tiny smudge of flour there. "Anything else you'd like me to do?"

"Nah, I think we've got everything under control. The mashed potatoes and rolls are done. The chicken will be ready in just a few minutes and Nina's got the salad and C.J.'s on lemonade duty."

"Is Aunt Ella still coming for dinner?" Nina glanced at the clock hanging on the wall over the kitchen sink. "She's late."

"You know Ella. She'll be late to her own funeral," Grace said of her older sister.

Malcolm checked to see if Nina was chopping the cucumber into proper slices. She wasn't, as far as he was concerned. "Make the rounds thinner, honey. It's garden salad, not cucumber salad."

Nina rolled her eyes but did as their father suggested. C.J. squeezed the juice from a lemon half inside a pitcher.

It was a typical dinner at the Davis household, but C.J. couldn't shake her preoccupation with Ethan Tanner. She thought about their last encounter in his shop. She'd shot out of there just when things were really starting to heat up between them. What rattled her wasn't just the pull of her body to his. She sensed there could possibly be more between her and Ethan than great sex. They'd have a lot in common. The thought that she could possibly want more than a good time was unsettling. That's why she'd hightailed it out of his shop that day. She needed time to think, get her bearings.

"So C.J., how's the work on the Barracuda coming?" her father asked.

"Moving along smoothly, Daddy," C.J. replied, willing herself to focus on the car, not the hunky shop owner. She reached for another lemon half and squeezed.

"Honey, we have something for that." Grace moved away from the hot skillet, rose up on her toes to reach inside a cabinet to remove a glass juicer. "Here." She placed it near the bowl of lemons. "This will strain the seeds and pulp, too."

Malcolm piped up, "Let C.J. make the lemonade the way she wants to, Grace."

"I don't like the seeds or the pulp," Nina said, but Malcolm ignored her comment.

"I hear you took it to Tanner's. Think they'll have the car done in time for the Dream Cruise?" Malcolm claimed a seat at the kitchen table where the ornate overhead lighting reflected off his balding head.

C.J. plucked a carrot to munch from the neat little piles of vegetables near Nina. "The shop's owner says it's not a problem." C.J. mashed a lemon half against the plastic top of the juicer and smiled at Nina, who smiled back and gave her a thumbs-up for taking her wishes into account regarding the lemonade.

"That is one of the better auto shops in town, but then, you must already know that or you wouldn't have trusted them with the car," her father said.

Looking over her shoulder, Grace said, "Just when I thought I was getting used to that trucking thing you do, here come the raggedy cars. I swear, C.J., sometimes I wonder . . ." Her words trailed off when Malcolm caught her eye with a warning look. She thought better of revealing the rest of what she intended to say.

"What, Mom? Just get it out. Go for it." For a change C.J. had been encouraged by her mother's refreshing candor, but Malcolm wasted no time cutting Grace off.

"If you're happy, sweetie," Grace replied with a sweet smile, "that's all that matters, of course."

Once again the curtain slammed down on candid communication with one of C.J.'s parents.

"That's right . . . as long as C.J.'s happy," Malcolm echoed cheerily.

Grace turned to give the skillet of chicken her full attention again.

C.J. gritted her teeth and darted a meaningful glance at Nina, who knew what she was feeling at that moment.

C.J. loved her parents with all her heart and knew they meant well. But there were still times when she cringed at what she felt was disingenuous and overly solicitous behavior. Old habits died hard and she supposed she couldn't blame them. Most of her family had spent years trying to compensate for the unfortunate hand C.J. had been dealt regarding her health.

"Chicken's ready," Grace broke into C.J.'s thoughts. She removed the meat from the skillet and placed it in a big ceramic bowl lined with thirsty paper towels.

The doorbell rang.

C.J. popped up from her chair. "I'll bet that's Aunt Ella. I'll get it."

Soon they were all gathered around a large mahogany table in the dining room enjoying their meal while Aunt Ella prattled on about her trip to an auto shop to get the muffler on her Camry replaced.

Ella, who looked a lot like Grace, without the fifties sitcom mom clothes, was particularly gregarious and animated that evening.

"I always get this sick feeling around mechanics. Many of them are such hucksters. Rip-off artists." Ella shuddered, then sank her fork into the mound of fluffy mashed potatoes on her plate. "I always feel as if they take one look at me and start licking their chops over how much they're going bilk out of me because I'm just an old woman daring to come in all alone to have some work done."

"Nonsense! You're not old, Aunt Ella," Nina said before taking a sip of lemonade.

"Old is a state of mind," C.J. added.

"Ella, why didn't you ask me or C.J. to go with you?" Malcolm filled his plate with salad.

"I didn't want to be a bother and I should handle my own business. Besides, it was just a muffler and I had a thirty-percent-off coupon to boot. But by the time they were done the bill was twice as much as what I'd expected to pay. And I'm now the owner of a whole spanking new exhaust system that I have this feeling I didn't need."

"Oh, Aunt Ella. I really wish you'd called me." C.J. reached across the table to pat her aunt's hand.

"I thought you were already back on the road, sweetie," Ella said.

"I do have a load that'll take me to Maine and then D.C., but that's been delayed, so I have a few more days in town before I have to take off," C.J. explained.

"Will you be here long enough to help me work the barbecue fest at Belle Isle this weekend?" Ella asked.

"Yeah, sure. I'm all yours."

"And what about you, Nina dear?" Ella teased Nina, well aware that the thought of ruining one of her cute outfits with a hickory smoke scent would be a turnoff for her.

Twisting her mouth in distaste, Nina responded just as expected: "Sorry, got other plans."

"We'll be there, of course. But not to report for duty." Malcolm chuckled. "We just want to people-watch, enjoy the bands—"

"And stuff our faces," Grace cut in with a big grin.

"Slackers. So it's just me and Aunt Ella," C.J. said. "What time should I show up on Saturday?"

"Well, if you get to my place by seven and we show up at the fest by eight a.m. for setup, we should be fine. Is that a problem?"

C.J. looked forward to spending time with her aunt. "No problem. Should be lotsa fun!"

8

It was a fabulous day for the annual Porkopolis B-B-Q Fest and Cookoff at Belle Isle. The sky was cloudless and a vibrant blue. The sun shone bright. Leaves danced on a light summer breeze. The temperature hovered around a comfortable seventy-six degrees. Hundreds of people picnicked around dozens of booths, where B-B-Q contestants busied themselves grilling, smoking, basting, and boiling.

At an assigned booth Ella worked her magic over four long slabs of ribs sizzling on an old barrel grill.

C.J., who had spent the last hour and a half helping Ella set up, relaxed on a lawn chair, tapping her feet as an R & B band on a nearby stage played a medley of old Motown hits. The scrumptious scent of well-seasoned meat teased her nose and made her stomach rumble.

Ella schooled her on Barbecue 101. "See, you want to have that smoked flavor, but you don't want to overdo it. Too much smoke can make the ribs taste bitter. Also, you have to let the meat cook for just the right amount of time. You want to strike a nice balance. You want the meat tender, but not too mushy."

"Right," C.J. would chime in here and there to let Ella know she was listening and taking mental notes.

"I think I've finally perfected my technique and I plan to place higher than third this year. I'm ready for those judges. Bring 'em on!" Ella cackled.

Approximately sixty competitors vied for three titles: Best Barbecue Ribs, Best Pork Shoulder, and Best Whole Hog.

C.J. stood and stretched. "Aunt Ella, I left my sunglasses in the truck. I'm gonna go fetch 'em. Be right back."

"Take your time, sweetie. Most of your work here is done until we pack it in for the day."

As C.J. strolled along the row of booths, she noticed that most contestants had painted silly names on homemade signs, then hung them high over their booths. First she encountered the Bastey Boys. A few feet down she peeked over at booths labeled Swine & Dine, Getting Piggy With It, and Aporkalypse Now. But it was the familiar male form at the booth labeled The Porkcrastinator that garnered more than her fleeting glance. None other than Ethan Tanner stood over a huge pit with a long two-pronged fork in his hand. Before she could think, her feet were carrying her in his direction.

He was so busy concentrating on the large hunk of meat simmering on his pit he didn't notice C.J. right away, but the older man with cheerful gray eyes and grizzled hair sitting next to him did. He cleared his throat. "Ethan, I think we have company."

"The Porkcrastinator, huh?" C.J. grinned up at Ethan. "Is that *you*?"

Ethan's face opened in a wide smile that showcased those perfect white teeth. "C.J.! What a pleasant surprise!" He placed his two-pronged fork on a small table, walked over to gather C.J. in his arms.

"Hi, Ethan." C.J. enjoyed the intimate and enthusiastic greeting. He embraced her as if they'd known each other for years.

"Don't tell me you're competing, too?" Ethan ended the hug but kept a possessive hand at the small of her back.

"Nah, I'm here helping my aunt Ella."

"If she's going for the Best Pork Shoulder title, she might as well go home right now, 'cause that title is mine," Ethan boasted good-naturedly.

"No, you two aren't going head-to-head, so my loyalties won't be split. She's competing in the Best Ribs category."

"Lucky for her." Ethan chuckled. "It's so good to see you. But hey, wait a minute. I thought you'd left town."

"That load I told you about got delayed a few days."

"And you didn't phone me?" Ethan brought his hand to a spot on his chest near his heart as if to indicate she'd crushed it.

"I was going to, but I happened upon you here."

"Fate," Ethan said, looking at her in a way that made her feel like the most desirable woman he'd ever encountered, though she was wearing another oversize T-shirt and roomy walking shorts that grazed her knees. She'd given the boots a rest that day and slipped on some sandals. Her feet didn't know what had hit them.

"So you're into this barbecue thing, huh?" she asked, tipping her head to one side.

The older man in the chair got up and offered C.J. his hand. "I'm Gus Tanner, this knucklehead's grandpappy."

"Hello. I'm C.J. Nice to meet you, Mr. Tanner."

"Call me Gus."

"I was just so surprised and pleased to see C.J. here, I forgot my manners," Ethan explained.

Gus clapped Ethan on the back. "You're forgiven. I can see how such a pretty face could distract a man."

C.J. felt the heat of a blush creep up from her neck to her cheeks. Between these two Tanner men a girl's head could swell to the size of a parade float.

"So you say you're here helping your aunt?" Gus asked.

"Yeah. She's just four booths down on the right."

"Hmmm, the portable restrooms are in that direction and I really need to go. I'll pass that booth on the way." Gus paused, then added, "So she's doing her thing on some ribs, you say?" A glint of interest lit his gray eyes as he smacked his lips. "I love what Ethan does with a pork shoulder, but a taste of some ribs sure would be a nice treat, too."

Ethan's face crumbled with mock hurt. "Traitor!"

C.J. laughed.

"Think she'd mind letting me sample some?" Gus waggled his unruly brows.

"She'd be flattered that you're interested. I can introduce you two," C.J. offered.

Before replying, Gus looked to Ethan, who was obviously not pleased with the idea of C.J. leaving so soon. "No, you stay right here with Ethan. He needs the company, 'cause he can't leave his shoulder unattended. Just tell me your aunt's name. I can introduce myself and then tell her you sent me."

C.J. hesitated, then agreed. Aunt Ella was a real people person in every sense of those words. She'd strike up a conversation with anyone anywhere, no formal introductions required. "Her name is Ella, fourth booth down on the right."

Gus took off, in that direction.

C.J. turned her attention to Ethan again.

Ethan offered C.J. a lawn chair. "So, now that my pitman is gone, I guess you'll have to pinch-hit."

"Pitman?"

"Yeah. The pitman tends to the fire. Don't worry.

I'll teach you everything you need to know if the fire falters."

C.J. nodded, then sat. She tugged at her beige Bermuda shorts. She had noticed that Ethan appeared to admire her legs before working his way up to her face.

He grabbed another lawn chair and placed it beside hers. "You look wonderful, by the way."

C.J. snorted and flapped a hand at him dismissively. "You're kiddin', right? These ol' rags?"

"I believe this is the first time I've seen you without blue jeans and your big black boots, which I find oddly sexy." He winked at her.

"Yeah, right," she scoffed, thinking he looked utterly swoon-worthy himself. The broad shoulders and muscular chest set off a trim midsection that flowed into powerful thighs and a round, tight butt that made C.J. want to take a big ol' bite out of him.

He wore navy knee-length cotton shorts that accentuated his slightly bowed legs, and a white short-sleeved pullover shirt. His strong-looking calves were sprinkled with the silkiest dark hair. The man was perfect from head to toe! Even his feet, which were tucked in brown leather huaraches, looked good to her. Her thoughts veered where they shouldn't in a public place. It was time to try to distract herself with small talk. "So, you're doing a pork shoulder?"

"Yup. Smoking it with hickory—pignut hickory, to be exact. Shoulders cook very slowly with indirect smoky heat," he said, scooting his chair closer to hers until their knees touched.

"Smoky heat, huh?" she managed, lost in his onyx eyes.

"The slower the burn the better." His voice went thick and low, causing C.J. to wonder if he was referring to the pit or *her*. After all, he had made her feel like one of the white-hot chunks of charcoal in his pit.

Ethan casually placed one arm around her shoulder and his skilled fingers dangled past a cotton sleeve and made contact with her skin. He drew soft circles there for a few seconds, then ventured upward to twirl the end of the ponytail around his fingers. "You have very pretty hair."

"Thanks," C.J. said, resisting the urge to tackle him right then and there. "Tell me more about this pignut hickory thing."

Ethan caressed the shell of her ear with a fingertip. "Charcoal alone just doesn't have the same flavor. Pignut hickory mixed in gives it that extra kick. Something about those two . . ." He paused, then whispered in her ear, "They're perfect together."

"I see."

"Like I suspect we could be."

"No doubt," C.J. replied, going with the flow.

"Wet or dry?" he suddenly asked.

This man's touches and thick whispers already had her damp and humming between the thighs. "Excuse me?"

"What I was trying to ask you is if you prefer a *wet sauce* or *dry rub*. Barbecue speak."

"Oh!" C.J. blinked, feeling foolish for reading a salacious meaning into his wet/dry question. Panty-scorching horniness, which she was experiencing that moment, could do that to a woman.

Ethan continued, "There are different schools of thinking when it comes to adding more flavor to the meat. Some people rub it down with dried spices for a powdery marinade."

"A rubdown sounds real good," she purred, her thoughts far from pig parts.

"And others prefer the wet approach with a sauce also made with various herbs and spices."

"Right," C.J. replied. "So what kind of seasoning do you prefer, Mr. Tanner?" She slanted him a co-quettish look.

Ethan's fingers continued to stroke a spot on her shoulder. "I prefer both, actually—a little bit of dry for initial marinating; then after the shoulder is nearly done I'll paint on a liquid concoction of the same herb mix. And I'm gonna let you in on the top-secret part of my recipe." He leaned toward her to whisper in her ear. The move caused little tingles to dance up her spine. "I inject the meat with a solution of vinegar and fruit juices to make it extra tender."

"You're already letting me in on all the details of your secret recipe and we hardly know each other," she teased.

"I'm sure that's going to change. The connection

we obviously have. . . . I'm enjoying it. I haven't felt this way about anyone in a while and wasn't sure I would ever again."

"Why me?" C.J. asked, surprised that she even cared enough to ask.

"You're . . . well . . . different. I love that."

Before she could respond, Gus returned to the booth. He licked his fingers and dabbed a napkin around his mouth to wipe away excess barbecue sauce. "You'd better be glad you're competing in the Shoulder category, because I do believe Ella would kick your ass, boy," he teased Ethan. "Oooh-wee! That woman put her foot in those ribs! That was some good eatin'! I'm glad you came by, C.J., or else I would've missed out."

"Yeah, Aunt Ella can burn all right. Ribs aren't her only specialty."

"I know, and she was quick to point that out, too," Gus said. "Invited me to dinner later this week."

C.J. didn't hide her surprise. "Oh, she did, did she?"

Ethan clapped his grandfather on the back. "Talkin' about working fast."

"Ella is a nice lady. *Very nice* in more ways than one." Gus moved to take a seat on a lawn chair. "There might be snow on the roof, but there's plenty of fire in the hearth. I still enjoy the company of a good-looking woman every chance I get."

"Sounds as if you and Aunt Ella clicked. That's nice." C.J. meant what she said and backed it up with a smile. She'd taken an instant liking to Ethan's grandfather.

"Yeah, clicking ain't just for you young folks, you know." Gus tossed meaningful looks at Ethan, then C.J.

"Ethan and I have a business relationship." C.J. thought she should clarify, though she had a feeling that would change soon. "I have a vehicle at his shop."

"Oh, so he hasn't gotten around to asking you out just yet?" Gus looked at Ethan. "Boy, what's taking you so long? I know you're not gonna to let your old grandpappy beat your time."

Ethan chuckled. "I'm working on it, Granddad. I'm working on it. C.J. here is one very busy young lady. She's a trucker."

"A trucker?" With his mouth agape, Gus looked to C.J. as if evaluating her with new eyes. "Get out of town!"

"And I plan to," C.J. added with wink at the older man. "I'm leaving for Maine in a couple of days."

"Well, I do declare. Live long enough and you see it all."

"But I haven't given up on trying to finagle a date with her," Ethan said to his grandfather before turning to C.J. again. "So how about it? Can you squeeze me in over the next two days?"

"Afraid not. Still got lots of things on my to-do list." C.J. was prolonging the inevitable, but a part of her didn't want to appear *too* easy or available.

Most men did appreciate a bit of mystery and challenge.

"Here we go with that list of yours again." Ethan looked disappointed.

"But I promise to give you a call when I return. Maybe we can work something out then."

"*Maybe?* Oooh, playing hard to get, huh?" Gus laughed. "Sounds like she's gonna make you wait and work real hard, Ethan."

Ethan kept his eyes on C.J. "And you know me, Granddad. I don't give up easily. I've even pulled out the big guns and shared the secret to my smoked shoulder recipe with her."

"Oooh-weee, now this *is* serious. He hasn't even told me what's in that concoction he injects in the meat with a turkey baster."

"So C.J., you still headed to D.C. after Maine?" Ethan took both of her hands in his.

"Yes."

"Me and the 'Cuda will be waiting when you get back."

It was then C.J. realized she'd been so wrapped up in what had been happening between her and Ethan, she hadn't even bothered to inquire about her precious car.

"So how is Gary doing with it?" she asked, casually removing her hands from Ethan's.

"It's coming right along on schedule. I know you'll be pleased. Of course, feel free to stop by the shop and check before you take off."

"No need. You say things are moving right along. I trust you and your team with the car," C.J. said. "Well, I'd better get back to Aunt Ella. I want to be there with her when the judges taste her entry."

"Once they wrap their lips around Ella's ribs there'll be no need to taste the other entries in her category," Gus predicted.

"It was good seeing you again, Ethan." C.J. reached out to shake Gus's hand, but he startled her by springing to his feet and tugging her into a quick hug and peck on the cheek. "And nice meeting you, too, Gus."

C.J. turned to leave the covered booth, still marveling over the joyfully uninhibited and affectionate manner of both Tanner men. As the unrelenting sun rays beat down on her, she recalled those sunglasses she'd failed to retrieve from her truck but headed back to her aunt's booth instead. C.J. brushed aside her concerns about getting too emotionally attached to Ethan. She wanted him in her bed and she aimed to have him. She would focus on that, because guys simply didn't come hotter. The forceful physical attraction cracking between them demanded action. Yes, she would ring his cell phone as soon as she returned to Detroit and she'd go out with him a few times. She owed that to herself.

day C.J. planned to keep busy with er- omehow she found herself pulling into Ethan's Southfield repair shop. So much for maintaining an air of mystery and not appearing too eager.

As she climbed out of her pickup, Sid spotted her. "Here to check on your car, I presume."

"Um, yeah." C.J. felt her cheeks flame with a blush as if Sid knew her priority was actually seeing Ethan. This little pit stop was so out of character for her, but she refused to think it to death. She liked Ethan. Wanting to see him before she took off for Maine was perfectly fine . . . as long as she didn't get too carried away.

"This way," Sid said as he led her to the service area where the Barracuda was stationed.

"Is the boss around by any chance?" C.J. asked casually as she moved to the car and opened the hood.

"Yeah, he's in his office. Want me to tell him you're here?"

"Think it would be all right if I went to him?" C.J. peered inside and saw that the repairs were moving along nicely.

"Go right ahead," Sid said. "His office is right through there." He pointed the way.

When C.J. reached the closed door to Ethan's office, she ran her hands over her hair, which was gathered up in a ponytail as usual. She tamed stray strands, then checked to make sure the edge of her T-shirt was tucked neatly inside her jeans. She'd worn her most flattering, good-butt jeans that day. Subconsciously she must have known she'd find a way to see Ethan though she'd told him she didn't have the time. She cupped her hand over her mouth and blew. The move was not the most reliable fresh-breath check so she reached inside her shoulder bag and popped a peppermint round for insurance, then knocked.

"Come in." Ethan's warm, rich baritone made her skin tingle and her belly flip. She couldn't remember ever having that reaction to any man. She'd lusted for guys before, but somehow this felt different.

When she opened the door and stepped inside, Ethan looked up from the papers on his desk and treated her to a smile that took up half of his face. "C.J.!"

"I, um, I," C.J. stammered, "hope you don't mind my dropping by without notice, see I was—"

"Mind? I think I willed you to appear, lady. I was having a hard time getting my work done because I was just thinking about you." He rose, then walked around his desk to her.

"About what you mentioned the other day . . ." C.J. startled a bit when Ethan moved close enough to take her hand and peck her cheek with a quick kiss that sent her heart rate on a tear. "The coffee and the car photos . . . I was in the neighborhood, thought I'd take you up on that offer if you have time. I know this is short notice and all so I'll understand if you can't." C.J. found herself babbling until Ethan placed a finger to her lips to silence her.

"It's all right, C.J. You have no idea how glad I am to see you. You're not intruding." He glanced at his wristwatch. "It's almost lunch time. I'll order something and have it delivered. What would you like?"

C.J. shrugged. "Whatever's convenient."

"That would be Cheetos and Mountain Dew from the vending machines." He moved to the phone on his desk. "Not quite what I had in mind. How does pizza sound?"

"Good."

He put the receiver to his ear and dialed. "The works?"

"Even better."

While they waited for their lunch, Ethan took out several thick photo albums of classic and custom cars Tanner's had serviced over the years. They sat on the small, but comfy sofa adjacent to the desk as Ethan shared a story about each vehicle. C.J. listened enraptured until they were interrupted by the pizza delivery guy.

Ethan paid the lanky teen for the pizza and tipped him generously. Soon they were alone again.

They settled back on the sofa with the hot pizza and cold soft drinks, then talked cars and trucks for another hour while they ate.

"So just how long have you been a gear head, my dear?" Ethan wanted to know.

"For as long as I can remember. When I was a little girl, I used to bury the dolls I got for Christmas in the backyard, then I'd tell my folks I lost them. Had no use for those things." C.J. scrunched up her face.

"Girl toys, except for bikes, were so boring back then, too. Snoozeville. I liked things that moved or had some real power or speed in them. I hung out with the boys on my block so I could play with their things—especially their Hot Wheels and battery-operated and remote-control cars."

"How did you manage that? When I was a boy, the gang I ran with would not have agreed to that. All girls were dumb and had cooties as far as we were concerned."

C.J. laughed. "I wasn't exactly welcomed with open arms at first. I had to bribe my way in."

"Oh, really? With what?"

"I had a pretty slammin' mounted bug collection so I got a whole lot of mileage out of that *and* Mom's homemade oatmeal raisin cookies. Those things were so melt-in-your-mouth delicious they were like gold. After the gang got to know me better, the leader, a boy named Jeffrey Pigues, I'll never forget him and his jet-black curly hair . . . and how he used to smell like grape Now and Laters all the time," C.J. said wistfully.

"Uh-oh, I think somebody had a crush."

"Maybe just an itty-bitty one." C.J. chuckled. "I was way more enamored with his Tonka truck stash if truth be told. Anyway, I digress, after Jeffrey announced that I was, and I quote, 'All right for a girl', I was in like Flynn from that moment on and bribes were no longer required."

Ethan studied her with a smile on his face. "And you're still all right . . . I mean, for a girl."

C.J. playfully punched his shoulder, then nestled closer as he wrapped an arm around her and placed a warm, lingering kiss on her forehead. She reached up and linked her fingers with his, then squeezed. "I guess you're all right, too . . . for a boy."

9

The next day, Ethan had just showered, shaved, and stepped into a pair of well-worn jeans when the doorbell rang. The clock on his bedroom nightstand read 7:43 a.m. He wasn't expecting anyone until 9:00 a.m., when Jacinda was scheduled to arrive to give him an update on Luminesque, the jewelry design business she and Leigh-Ann had started together.

The two women had been best friends since high school, and when Jacinda moved into a condo complex just two blocks from the old Farmington Hills home Ethan and Leigh-Ann used to share, she became his friend, too.

Ethan had sold that house three months ago and moved into a loft condo, and he didn't see Jacinda as often. When Leigh-Ann was alive rarely a day passed when the two women didn't see or speak to each other. Leigh-Ann's and Hailey's deaths had hit Jacinda just as hard as they had Ethan and the family.

Ethan finished securing the fly of his jeans, stepped into some leather sandals, then reached inside a chest of drawers to remove a black T-shirt, which he pulled over his head, then tugged over his lean torso.

At the front door he pushed a button that would allow Jacinda entry into his building and waited. When Jacinda got off the elevator down the hall he noticed the two plastic grocery bags in her arms. "Hey, I thought we'd agreed on nine a.m. You're early."

Jacinda stepped inside the foyer with her shoulder-length brown curls bouncing and good cheer glowing on her tawny heart-shaped face. "I know. I hope you don't mind."

He welcomed her with a warm smile and a quick hug.

"What's all this?" Ethan claimed both bags to lighten her load.

"I was going to stop by Starbucks for coffee and Panera's for bagels and cream cheese, but I thought something more substantial would be nicer while we talk." Jacinda removed her lightweight red jacket, then kept moving toward the kitchen with Ethan on her heels.

Ethan took the jacket and quickly hung it in a closet.

At the black granite-topped island in the kitchen she removed all the fixings for a hearty breakfast from the bags—bacon, eggs, grits, fruit salad, maple syrup, orange juice, milk, coffee, pancake mix.

"You didn't have to go to all the trouble, Cinda. The coffee and bagels would've been just fine." Ethan settled on one of the stools circling the island.

"I did worry about intruding this time of morning," she said. "Then I thought it might be OK because I know you're an early riser, too. But I must confess this isn't a completely altruistic gesture. I woke up this morning with a monster craving for a tall fluffy stack of pancakes, my specialty. Thought you could use a treat, too." Jacinda shoved the orange juice inside the refrigerator. "Where do you keep your mixing bowls and utensils these days?"

Ethan pointed to the location at the end of a row of cherrywood cabinets. She plucked the necessary cookware from the expensive set of gourmet pots and pans dangling from a rack mounted on the ceiling above the island.

"We'll have plenty of time for our breakfast meeting about Luminesque before we have to leave for Beatrice's," Jacinda said.

Ethan, Jacinda, and Whitmore family members on the committee were scheduled to meet at Beatrice's West Bloomfield home later that morning to discuss plans for the gala they were organizing for a college scholarship fund in Leigh-Ann's memory. The scholarship would benefit underprivileged high school students interested in pursuing careers in art, a project Leigh-Ann had started just before the tragic car accident.

Leigh-Ann had been a gifted artist, who expressed her immense talent through oil paintings, sculptures, and jewelry design. She and Jacinda, who also had a degree in art, gave up more lucrative careers in advertising to launch Luminesque five years ago, when they first started trekking to accessories trade shows on the weekends hoping to land jewelry design or jewelry vendor's contracts with national retailers. Their extensive collection included tiaras, combs, earrings, chignon holders, and bracelets.

Ethan had inherited Leigh-Ann's portion of the business. Because he knew nothing about jewelry design and had little interest in it, he'd assumed Jacinda would make him a buyout offer soon after Leigh-Ann died, but she hadn't. Whenever he had broached the subject, Jacinda advised him against making a major decision about selling so soon. The last time he mentioned selling his interest was six months ago.

Jacinda washed her hands in the sink, then proceeded to open the box of pancake mix. She poured some into a measuring cup she'd found in a cabinet.

"I can make myself useful, too." Ethan started the coffee machine, then reached overhead for a skillet to fry the bacon. "So what's the latest on Luminesque?" he asked to get their business meeting going.

Jacinda dumped the contents of the measuring cup inside a big ceramic bowl, then added eggs and milk. "I think the tiaras Leigh-Ann designed are going to be a huge hit for us."

Ethan recalled that Leigh-Ann had been so proud of those headpieces. Though he couldn't tell a Swarovski crystal from the run-of-the-mill rhinestone, he had listened patiently as she chattered about the materials she'd used to create the tiaras.

Ethan removed the electric griddle from a bottom cabinet, placed it on the counter, and plugged its cord in a power outlet.

"I have some new designs, spreadsheets, and bank statements I'd like you to see, but my arms were so full with the bags, I left my briefcase in the car. I'll go get it after we've eaten." Jacinda stirred the ingredients in her bowl vigorously. "So how have you been holding up?"

"Good. Of course, I'll always miss Leigh-Ann and Hailey, but I realize Leigh-Ann would want me to move on, so I'm trying to do that."

"I miss her, too." Jacinda's features softened into a melancholy expression. "She was like a sister to me."

Ethan wore a sentimental grin. "I know. I've always marveled at you two, wondering how you could find so much to yak about day in and day out."

"Some mornings I still wake up and I immediately reach for the phone on the nightstand because I want to gossip with her about something, then . . . I realize I just can't call her up to chat anymore."

"I hear you. It's the littlest things, even the annoying stuff you'd always taken for granted, that you miss the most about Leigh-Ann and Hailey . . . like finding Hailey's Barbies wedged between the cushions of my favorite chair or her sticky finger-prints on the bathroom walls," Ethan said softly. He watched the bacon sizzle in the skillet, but a smiling Hailey flashed through his mind and made his heart squeeze powerfully as always.

"When you say 'move on,' you mean beyond sell-ing the Farmington Hills house and buying this place?" Jacinda's question interrupted his daydream. She tested the griddle, then poured three perfect cir-cles of batter on its surface.

Ethan was referring to not only his choice of resi-dence but his love life as well. He'd been celibate since Leigh-Ann died and he hadn't realized how much he missed the company of a woman until re-cently. C. J. Davis and the feel of her delectable curves in his arms came to mind, but he didn't intend to share that information with anyone who was close to Leigh-Ann just yet. Too awkward. He wondered if he'd ever feel comfortable talking about another woman to Leigh-Ann's friends and family. He still needed to adjust to the idea himself. The moving-on attitude was still fairly new to him.

Jacinda continued adding to a leaning stack of golden-brown rounds as Ethan finished frying the bacon.

"I loved that house," he said. "But when the op-portunity to move into this place fell into my lap, I had to go for it. There were some great memories in my old home, so giving it up wasn't easy, but it was making the process of getting on with things extremely difficult."

"But it seems as if you're going all out to distance yourself." Jacinda looked around the slick, sophisticated interior of his kitchen, which boasted the latest state-of-the-art stainless-steel appliances, ultra-modern kitchen furnishings, and an exotic Brazilian cherrywood floor.

"Yeah, I suppose. Sometimes a fresh start can mean going in a completely different direction."

"You can't get more polar opposite than this place," Jacinda said in a tone that almost sounded as if she didn't approve of his new home.

True, his new place, which had come fully furnished, was nothing like where he'd lived until just three months ago. The home he'd shared with his wife and daughter was a more family-oriented New England colonial–inspired structure, nestled on a quaint birch-lined street. It had a front porch, a huge family room, and a sprawling backyard where Hailey romped on a swing set, splashed in a vast inground pool, and had tea parties with her dozens of dolls in the giant dollhouse Ethan had built. Ethan also had his own bricked play area equipped with an expensive grill specially designed for one of his favorite pastimes, barbecuing.

He used to live for those weekend cookouts when he'd invite all of their friends and family over for a feast. He hadn't thrown a party since he lost

Leigh-Ann and Hailey, and a big barbecue blowout would be difficult to have in his new, more contemporary digs which screamed "bachelor pad!" Most of the building's residents were thirty-something single six-figure-earning professionals on the career fast track.

His four-thousand-square-foot condominium took up half of a floor in the twelve-story building. The condo's furnishings were modern and sleek.

Jacinda placed the platter of hot pancakes on the table. Ethan set a plate of crispy bacon and a pot of hot coffee beside them while Jacinda removed the juice from the refrigerator.

Before they settled at the table Ethan got plates, glasses, cloth napkins, and silverware. "I'm still interested in selling my part of Luminesque to you, Cinda. You don't need me slowing you down."

"But you're not slowing things down," she said, helping herself to three pancakes and three pieces of bacon.

Ethan filled their glasses with juice. "How can I not slow you down? We've been meeting every three weeks now for the last few months just so you can let me look over business plans, designs, and spreadsheets that I have absolutely no expertise or interest in, if truth be told. Besides, I'm thinking about starting a second business that's more in line with the auto repair and body shops. If you feel you must have a partner, I suggest you approach Leigh-Ann's mother. I can talk to her, feel her out to see if she's interested in helping you. Maybe not the designing; that would be your area of expertise, of course. But I'm sure Beatrice would be a whiz at budgeting, marketing/promotion, you know, the business side of things. She'd be way better suited than I am, 'cause she's a woman interested in those froufrou bangles, baubles, and beads things that you're hawking."

At that suggestion a frown tugged at Jacinda's neatly arched brows and she pursed her glossed lips into a tight knot.

"Is there a problem?" Ethan was confused by her reaction. "I know Beatrice adores you, Cinda. I think she'd be pleased to help you with the business you started with her daughter. It's the perfect solution."

"I'm sure you do think it's perfect." Jacinda's response sounded like an accusation.

"And what's *that* supposed to mean?"

"Isn't it obvious?"

"No, but I'm sure you're going to tell me." Ethan knew he wouldn't like where this conversation was headed.

Jacinda paused and sighed. "Well . . . ," she said, now looking more solemn than annoyed. "It's as if you're . . . you're . . . trying to erase, cut, or change *everything* that has anything to do with Leigh-Ann and Hailey."

"What?" Ethan could feel the muscles in his jaw working. "That's not fair and I can't believe you think that."

"I can't believe how you've changed. They haven't been gone all that long."

"It's been a year and a half, Jacinda. And the length of time one spends mired in self-pity, suffering, unable to get out of bed in the morning is not directly proportional to the love you feel for that person who passed away. I still ache. I still grieve down deep because of those losses, but I still have every right—"

"I know, I know, to get on with your life," she droned in a mocking way.

That was the last straw as far as Ethan was concerned. "Look, Jacinda." He paused to measure his words, to really think about what he was about to say. "I know you loved Leigh-Ann and Hailey. I know you're still suffering, too, but you're out of line. And you have no right to judge me or my decisions." He could barely contain his anger as he scraped his chair away from the table and came to his feet.

"Your breakfast . . ." Jacinda seemed stunned by his reaction. What had she expected?

Ethan tossed his napkin on the table. "I'm not hungry anymore."

Jacinda's brown eyes clouded with remorse. "But—"

"Look, I have some things I need to take care of before I take off for that meeting at Beatrice's. Show yourself out when you're done," he said just before stalking out of the kitchen, leaving Jacinda alone with the bountiful breakfast.

• • •

C.J.'s latest road trip required hauling a load of computer systems. She drove her pickup truck to Farelli's Grocery Store, where she kept her semi in a space at the back lot.

She climbed inside the cab. The cinnamon scent of the potpourri air freshener dangling from a sun visor flap welcomed her to her home for the next few days. She placed her bags in the sleeping quarters, then settled on the cushioned front seat. She secured her seat belt, started the engine, then quickly scanned the dashboard's dials which could signal trouble with temperature, water, fuel, pressure, axles, electricity. She smoothed the soft red and white plaid flannel shirt she always placed over the backrest of the passenger side, which made it appear as if someone else were riding with her. Just a little safety tip she'd picked up from another female trucker. As she pulled the truck away from Farelli's, she looked up at the clear blue sky and wondered if the sunny weather would hold out. She ignored the tugging feeling she always experienced when she had to say good-bye to her family for days, sometimes weeks, at a time.

She'd merged with highway traffic to head toward the designated location to pick up her load. It wasn't long before the truck was on the interstate bound for Orono, Maine.

10

The white-eyed zombies came at Ethan from every direction. Legions of the undead with bloody, gaping wounds and mouthfuls of sharpened incisors popping on his computer screen as his swift fingers worked the keyboard as if his very life depended it.

"Whoa!" Ethan bellowed as the thundering *boom!* and *bang!* felt as if they would propel him from his seat. He was so engrossed in the Doom 3 video game he almost didn't realize the ringing of his desk phone wasn't part of the game's sound effects. He'd considered letting the answering machine pick it up, but curiosity got the best of him when caller ID displayed a cell phone number. A cell phone number he didn't recognize.

Still distracted, Ethan reached for the receiver, then tucked it between a shoulder and an ear so he could continue his assault on his keyboard. "Hello!" he said.

"Ethan, is that you?"

He could barely hear the female voice. "Yeah, and this is . . . ?"

"C.J."

That got his full attention. His fingers froze over the keyboard. "C.J.! It's so good to hear from you."

More shrieks and wails, booms and bangs, from the PC.

"What the hell is going on over there? What's all that noise?" she asked.

Ethan chuckled as he lowered the PC's volume, unsure whether he should reveal that though he was a grown man he still had a serious obsession with video games, especially the horror variety. He had been into the games—the arcade variety—since junior high. The more monsters, guts, and gore a game had in it, the better. "That's . . . um . . . Doom 3." He decided to come clean. If things worked out the way he hoped and he and C.J. got to be close, she'd find out about this particular pastime anyway.

"Doom 3? As in the video game?"

"You know it?" Ethan leaned back his chair, rolled it a few inches away from the desk so he could prop his Nikes on top.

"Yeah."

"Really?"

"Yup. That must be some tricked-out computer you have there, because that game requires some serious hardware."

"We're talking a Pentium 4 processor or its equivalent, five hundred megabytes of RAM, and a graphics card with at least two hundred and fifty-six megabytes of memory to really appreciate," he boasted.

"My computer is not so loaded, so I plan to purchase the Xbox format of that game first chance I get."

"You have Xbox?"

"Yup."

Ethan didn't feel self-conscious anymore. "I think I should let you know that a part of me will always have the taste of the gawky, pimply-faced teenage geek I used to be."

"You? A gawky, pimply-faced teenage geek? I can't picture that and nothing you can say can convince me."

"I'll let you in on another secret. I watch *Pimp My Ride* on MTV."

"No!" C.J.'s laughter bounced through the phone line.

"So when are you coming back home?"

It had been two and a half weeks since he last saw C.J. and that time had dragged like a month.

"I'm in D.C., calling to check on my car. The Dream Cruise is just a little over a week away, as I'm sure you know."

"Just checking in on the car, huh?" Ethan asked, unabashedly fishing for more.

"Checking on the car and . . . *you*." C.J.'s voice dropped to a seductive smokiness that caressed his ear.

"Well, the car is not quite done, but it will be soon. Don't worry. But me, I'm more than ready . . . to see you again."

"I can hardly wait."

"So you're heading back when?"

"Tomorrow."

Ethan looked skyward and silently mouthed the words, *Thank you*.

"So where are you staying in D.C.?"

"In my rig, of course, at a truck stop. This stop is one of the better ones and for once there was space to park. Their parking shortages are notorious, but it has showers, a decent restaurant, and postage facilities. In my truck I have a sleeper area and plenty of space for a little TV, a closet, and a fridge."

Ethan reached for the tennis ball on the desk and began a game of catch with the wall. He idly pitched the ball against the same spot on the plaster so it would bounce back at an arc that made it easy to catch without removing his feet from the desk. "A real home away from home, huh?"

"Exactly."

"Doesn't the loneliness get to you sometimes?"

Such a long silence stretched between them, Ethan wondered if they'd lost their connection. He anchored his feet and gave the ball a rest. "C.J.? Are you there?"

"Yeah, I'm still here."

Ethan could tell he'd put her on the spot, so he backed off. "I suppose even dream jobs have their drawbacks."

"True," C.J. replied.

Ethan thought it best to get straight to the point before he said something else that might stall their pleasant conversation. "So when can I see you again? If you don't have any plans this weekend—"

"You're on."

Her swift reply brought Ethan up short and left him momentarily speechless. He was finally making some real progress with her.

"What would you like to do?" she asked.

"Anything."

"Where would you like to go?"

"Anywhere."

They laughed. Ethan knew there was a chance his own overeagerness could prove to be a turnoff, but he was never into playing games or faking indifference. He was all about cutting the crap whenever possible. If he'd learned anything from losing Leigh-Ann and Hailey, it was that life was just too short for BS.

He was into C.J. and wanted to make sure she knew it.

"How about we both think about it and I'll give you a call Friday night when I'm scheduled to return to Detroit?"

"That'll work."

They chatted for another hour, until C.J. yawned and said sleepily, "Well, dude, I'm gonna go flatline now."

"What?" Ethan said with a note of alarm. He'd watched episodes of *ER* and flatlining was never good.

"Climb into my sleeper to turn in for the night," C.J. clarified with a chuckle.

"Oh! Sweet dreams then," he added with a smile on his lips.

"Um, well, sweet dreams to you, too," she replied as if it were the corniest thing that had ever crossed her lips, but she said it anyway.

That warmed Ethan. When he hung up the phone he was in no mood to continue his attack on an army of shrieking zombies. He had three days to plan what he hoped would be an unforgettable first official date with C.J.

11

Early Saturday morning Ethan pulled his custom 1947 International pickup truck he'd christened Betsy Blue into C.J.'s driveway. C.J. stepped outside her brick ranch house to greet him. She wore blue jeans, a red T-shirt, and a big smile that warmed Ethan from the inside out. Her hair was released from its usual thick elastic band and allowed to bounce in soft, shiny waves about her shoulders. Her tote bag was slung over one shoulder, and a garment bag flopped over the other. They were going to spend the entire day together. Finally! He'd been cryptic about the details of their date. He only instructed her to dress casually and comfortably for the day but bring along a dressier outfit for their evening.

"Hey, that was quick. You must've been jamming those gears," C.J. said.

Ethan had phoned ten minutes before to check the directions to her place that he'd gotten off the Internet. "I was already halfway here when I called from my cell." He stepped out of his truck, thinking she looked more gorgeous than he remembered.

"Whoa! So Beauty is all yours?" C.J. ogled his truck with slack-jawed wonder.

"Yes." Ethan puffed out his chest, so thrilled that she was impressed with his work.

"I didn't know you dabbled in radical customs, too!" C.J. whistled as she admired the classic truck's many features.

"I try to think outside the box. Something will pop up in my head; no matter how crazy or wild it seems at first on paper, I can usually make it work, with a little help from my mechanics and bodywork guys."

"Slick. Very slick." C.J. grinned and nodded, not taking her eye off the vehicular work of art.

"So this was one of your visions, huh? Right down to the corn silk blue paint?"

"Yup. Her name's Betsy Blue."

"I love it," C.J. said, slowly bobbing her head with approval.

"It took me seven long years to find a '47 International; then it took two additional years to get my hands on all the right parts, then another to put it together . . . with the help of my experts at the shop."

"You've gotta let me peek at that engine before we take off."

Ethan checked his wristwatch. "Well, we are running just a bit late—"

"Pleaassse, Ethan. You can't tease me like this, then leave me hanging. I'm dying to see it."

"Oh, all right, but we do have to get going—"

"Where are we headed anyway? You've been so secretive about the plans. Don't you think you oughta let me in on them now?"

"Patience, my child." He winked. "All will be revealed to you soon. Very soon."

Ethan walked to the hood and lifted it. "It's powered by a highly modified Chevy three-fifty."

"That's hot!" C.J. praised as she peered inside for a few minutes.

Ethan hurried her along. "You can admire it for as long as you like later." He cut off her view of the engine, then ushered her to the passenger side.

She was still taking in the truck's many assets when the tires caught her eye. "Hey, are those Boyd billet tires on here?"

"Yup." Ethan took her garment bag and helped her inside.

Once they were both settled in and seat-belted, he started the engine.

"So where are we off to?"

Ethan merely replied with a sly grin.

. . .

A half hour later they were parked at a small airport in a northwestern Detroit suburb.

"We're headed out of town?" C.J. asked.

"I hope that's not a problem. It's not an overnight trip. We'll return later this evening. I wanted to make sure of it. That's why we're flying private instead of commercial." Ethan helped her out of the truck, then reached back inside for their garment bags.

Soon they were taking off heading for the destination Ethan hoped would thrill his date.

The flight was short. It seemed as if they'd ascended and leveled off for about a half hour when the plane was suddenly descending.

Only after they touched down at a small airport on the outskirts of Chicago did he inform C.J. where they were.

A driver was waiting for them when they entered the airport. He led them both out to a black Town Car.

"Are we going where I think we're going?" C.J. smiled as if she already had a clue.

Ethan grinned and reached for her hand. "You'll see in due time."

The Great Midwestern Auto Show and Auction had been in full swing for two days when C.J. and Ethan arrived.

"This is too cool!" C.J. crowed when she got her first peek at the signs leading to ground zero, the convention center and fairgrounds.

Ethan instructed their driver when and where to return to pick them up later; then hand in hand they rushed inside the convention center like the rabid gearheads that they were.

The popular auto event had something for vehicle enthusiasts of every ilk. On hand for gawking or hawking were muscle cars, sport compacts, race cars, hot rods . . . wild and even wilder customs. Transportation that zoomed, boomed, zipped, and dipped was there for all to behold.

"I feel like a kid in a candy store!" C.J. fanned herself with the hand not holding Ethan's. She was practically hyperventilating with joy. Her head snapped in every direction as she tried to take it all in at once.

Ethan chuckled. "Careful! You're going to give yourself whiplash. And don't forget to breathe."

"I don't know where to look first!"

"I do." Ethan kept a firm hold on her hand, because he'd missed her while she was away and wanted to maintain as much physical contact as possible. It made him feel good that she didn't seem to mind.

He went to the information booth where four workers passed out glossy brochures and flyers with the times and locations of events and displays. Ethan quickly scanned one. "This way." He tugged her to the right. They weaved their way through a thick crowd of spectators and passed several booths and vehicles perched on platforms that caught C.J.'s eye.

"Hey, they even have crotch rockets here. Sssswweet!"

"Huh?"

"Crotch rockets."

When Ethan still didn't have a clue she clucked her tongue. "*Motorcycles,* dude," C.J. cracked, shaking her head, then replied playfully, "I'm gonna school you yet."

"Later for those. I think you'll want to get a loada this right now," Ethan said.

"What is it?"

"You'll see."

About ten booths down, C.J. stopped in her tracks and stared. "That's not what I think it is, is it?"

Ethan nodded, sure his satisfaction showed on his face.

"Do you know how long I've been wanting to see this baby?"

That "baby" was a totally radical custom car dubbed Purple Passion by its owner. The deep purple vehicle, a 1970 Plymouth Barracuda, was so over-the-top, it looked like something someone had sketched while cruising through a hallucinogenic drug trip. The show-stealing machine had earned its owner a slew of trophies on the auto show circuit. It had been splashed across the pages of several major classic and custom car publications out there.

C.J. removed her hand from Ethan's and read the

brochure. "Says here that it has an air-ride suspension, powered by a nine-hundred-horsepower, supercharged, five-hundred-and-forty-cubic-inch stroker motor. Whoa!"

"Whoa indeed," Ethan replied as they exchanged smiles. "Did I do good? Bringing you here on a first date?"

"Good? You did damn *great*. Thank you, Ethan," she said in a low voice that he still managed to hear over the noisy crowd. Her almond-shaped brown eyes shone with gratitude as she took his hand again. "But you know what the best part is? Besides being here, I mean."

"What?"

"The best part is you don't make me feel like some freak . . . or like I have a screw loose for actually enjoying all of this."

"Look at all the people around you, babe. You're hardly alone."

"Yeah, but the men outnumber the women by the dozens, in case you haven't noticed. You make me feel as if it's OK to be me."

"And why wouldn't I?" Ethan scanned her face, then moved to the red T-shirt, which skimmed her delicate shoulders, the soft swells of her breasts, and her trim waist. "You, or rather the bits of the real C.J. that you've revealed to me so far, are pretty fascinating. I can't wait to peel back more layers."

Amid the bustle of the auto show they stood there as a sensual intensity that could make scalding lakes of polar ice caps whirled around them. He reined in thoughts of removing the red cotton and blue denim barriers from her body. "Shall we continue our tour of this place?"

"Yes, let's!" C.J. said eagerly. "After we're done here with Purple Passion, I spotted a to-die-for 1964 Impala I think we should give another look."

As they approached Purple Passion for closer inspection, he noticed C.J. had nudged closer to him and curled one arm around his waist. He in turn curled an arm around hers. They took in the rest of the car show and auction just like that, linked side by side like a long-time loving couple who finished each other's sentences and anticipated each other's needs before they were verbalized.

Ethan inhaled deeply, savoring the scent of her strawberry-scented shampoo and feel of her curvaceous body. Leigh-Ann had been the love of his life, but from what he could tell so far, she and C.J. were as different as night and day. Yet his initial attraction to C.J. was as equally strong as what he'd felt when he first met Leigh-Ann.

Some people spent a lifetime looking for *the one,* someone they thought they could bond with on a soul-deep level. He'd found that with Leigh-Ann. After her death, he'd assumed that any other woman to come into his life would be a pleasant distraction at most. But C.J. was turning out to be so much more.

12

Their driver returned to the convention center and fairgrounds a little after 6:00 p.m. He drove them to an upscale Chicago neighborhood with sprawling homes and sweeping green lawns.

"My best friend, Rico, and his wife, Marisol, own this home. They're out of town for the weekend, but I have an open invitation to come here and make myself at home while we're here in Chicago." Ethan helped C.J. out of the car and ushered her up the stairs that led to the front door.

The driver removed their garment bags from the trunk and joined them on the stairs.

"I thought we could use a place to relax a bit, shower, and change clothes before the second phase of our date begins," Ethan said.

C.J. had had a blast at the auto show. "The second phase, huh?" She took her garment bag from the driver. "The first phase was pretty spectacular. Might be impossible to top."

"But I'm gonna give it a good shot." Ethan checked his watch. He turned to the driver and took his own garment bag from him. "I'd like you to return in . . . oh . . . about three hours."

"Sure thing." The driver saluted, then made his way back to the car and drove off.

"I'll be right back. I have to go next door to get the spare key." Ethan strode across the lawn to the equally impressive home to the left.

C.J. admired the beauty of the elaborate floral design popping with bright primary colors and the well-manicured lawn that surrounded the house. A few minutes later Ethan returned jingling a set of keys.

"I was told we could help ourselves to anything in the fridge. So if you're hungry—"

"I'm fine. All those hot dogs we ate at the auto show will tide me over until dinner."

Ethan slipped the key inside the lock, then opened the door and let C.J. enter first.

"They gave me a temporary code to disengage the alarm system, but looks as if they forgot to turn it on," he said.

C.J. stepped inside and scanned the foyer area. "This place is gorgeous. Your friends must be rich."

"They do well. As you can see, it's not a cozy

little cottage, but it's much homier than some impersonal hotel room. Would you like something to drink?"

"A cola would be nice," C.J. said out of habit until she remembered Dr. Meeks's orders about laying off the caffeine. "Make that fruit juice or lemonade if they have some."

"The kitchen's this way." Ethan turned left and C.J. followed him inside the gleaming state-of-the-art kitchen, heavy on rich pine and ceramic tiles.

He removed a can of cola from the refrigerator for himself and a can of apple juice for C.J. When he passed it to her his hand grazed hers, setting off small sparks. They'd spent most of the time at the auto show linked hand in hand or arm in arm, but now that they were alone the most fleeting touches felt loaded with sensual promise. Her body seemed to sizzle with longing as she admired his full lips. Ethan really was a beautiful and sexy man. How long had it been since she'd enjoyed wrapping herself around hard muscle and sinew? How long had it been since she'd opened herself up enough to let desire sweep her away, if only for a few hours?

She noticed the contrast between the heat from her hand wrapped around the chilled can.

They looked into each other's eyes and Ethan moved closer. C.J. tried to speak around the lump forming in her throat. "I heard you tell the driver to return in three hours. What do we do in the meantime?"

Ethan placed his can on top of the cabinet counter and did the same with hers. Her face was level with the hard mounds of his sculpted chest. He used a finger to lift her chin, then lowered his face to hers. Both hands then clamped around her waist. He tentatively touched his mouth to hers. The tip of his tongue traced a sweet damp line along her lips.

She soon parted her lips to allow him deeper access. Eager tongues merged and instantly moved in a matching rhythm that simulated the give and take, the charge and retreat, of passionate sex. She was hungry. Utterly starved. And he tasted spicy and downright delicious. Ethan drew her closer. He tipped her head to one side to deepen the kiss and slammed her against him. C.J. came up on her toes to wrap her arms around his neck.

Ethan coaxed the edge of her T-shirt out of her jeans and slipped one large hand underneath. He tugged a satin stretch fabric away from a plump breast and molded his hand around it. C.J. enjoyed the delicate scrapes of his callused palm against her pebbled nipple. With delectably firm pressure he kneaded her flesh, eliciting a moan of pleasure from her. Their lips stayed connected as they both feasted without inhibition. Now wet and throbbing to be fulfilled, she felt her brain go nearly blank. All she knew was she wanted him, and the evidence of how much he wanted her jabbed relentlessly against her soft middle. The heel of her hand met his hardness, tracing its contours, becoming familiar with its breadth and length. His mouth left hers for a moment and a husky groan of lust escaped. C.J. snatched the edge of Ethan's T-shirt from his jeans. Her fingers roamed over the curves and ridges of rock-hard muscle on his chest and back. They took brief reprieves from frenetic tongue tangling to fumble with the button and zippers on each other's blue jeans as the sounds of their labored breathing filled the room. They couldn't get the pants off fast enough; then C.J. heard something crash to the floor in the foyer.

Both froze.

"What was that?" C.J.'s head snapped in the direction from which the noise came. "I think someone else is here."

Shirtless, Ethan tipped toward the kitchen's entrance with C.J. on his heels. They peeked around the corner and saw an old woman Ethan didn't recognize. Her wide eyes flashed with embarrassment. It looked as if she had been trying to leave the house undetected but had tipped over the coatrack near the door in the process.

"Who are you?" Ethan closed the distance between himself and the older woman.

"I'm Hillary, the new housekeeper for the Lopezes." Hillary licked her lips and darted nervous looks at Ethan and C.J. "And I know you're the weekend guests they were expecting to use their home while they're away."

"I don't recall Rico and Marisol mentioning that you would be here," Ethan said, his expression hard.

"I'm not some thief. Um, well, uh . . ." Hillary swallowed and stammered, "I-I just spilled a bit of Ajax on my black pants here." She tapped at her thigh where a powdery patch of white and light greenish residue clung. "I was busy cleaning the half bathroom in the family room when I heard you two come inside. I didn't have time to put away all of my cleaning supplies, so I shoved some of them inside the entertainment center next to the Lopezes' CD collection."

No burglars would take the time to clean and scrub when they were in the middle of a heist, so C.J.'s gut told her this woman was definitely no criminal. Ethan must have believed Hillary, too, because now he relaxed his confrontational stance. Only then did he notice he was not only standing there bare chested, but his fly was ripped open, revealing a swatch of black briefs and a noticeable bulge, which reminded C.J.— *yikes!* She looked down at her own rumpled red T-shirt, then realized Ethan wasn't the only one whose jeans gaped open in the front. The bright white of her panties peeked out between the V formed by her own parted zipper. She felt her face flush as she turned to close it. For Ethan the task was not so simple. Instead he reached for a magazine in the stack of mail piled on a small table sitting near a wall in the foyer and used it to shield the view of his open fly. "Why were you trying to sneak out? Why didn't you let us know you were here?"

Hillary wrung her hands and shifted from one foot

to the other. "Well, you see, I've only had this job for two months and I've had some family problems, emergencies that have interfered with the schedule the Lopezes set for me. So far they've been nice and understanding about my tardiness and my failures to show when I was supposed to work. This weekend . . . well, I was supposed to come over and thoroughly clean the place yesterday afternoon, right after they took off for their weekend trip to Vegas, but . . ." She looked away from Ethan, then down at her hands.

"But what?" Ethan said more gently.

"I had another emergency. You see, my great-grandson's ill and I couldn't get anyone to babysit him yesterday. And he was in no condition for me to bring him with me, so I figured I'd come over early this morning, when I thought I could draft a neighbor to keep an eye on him. I thought I could get all my cleaning done this morning, long before you two got here, but—"

"But things didn't work out that way, right?" C.J. asked, feeling compassion for the frightened old woman.

Hillary's words rushed out in a desperate jumble: "I'm all little Cory has. And it's so hard and expensive to get reliable child care these days. Money's so tight. I really need this job. I can't lose this job. If the Lopezes found out I didn't have the house ready for you and that I was still here when you arrived, it might be the last straw. Please don't tell them."

Ethan made no promises, but C.J. could tell he

also felt empathy for the woman. "Go ahead and do what you need to do," he said instead.

"Meaning I can finish cleaning, while you're here?" Hillary tried to clarify.

"Yes." Ethan turned to C.J. "You don't mind, do you?"

"Of course not," C.J. piped up.

"It might take a while," Hillary said.

"I imagine it will; this place is huge," Ethan said.

"Bless you both! Praise God." Hillary exhaled a sigh of relief. She bent to pick up the fallen coatrack, then scurried away, disappearing into one of the other rooms.

"That was strange," C.J. said, shaking her head.

"Sorry about that." Ethan placed the magazine back on the small table, then secured his pants.

"No need to apologize. That poor woman . . ." C.J. turned toward the direction in which the housekeeper had disappeared. "She looked terrified. You're not going to tell your friend Rico she was still here when we arrived, are you?"

"No, I don't think so. She might be scamming us about the sick kid and babysitter woes and all, but I think I should let Rico and Marisol discover Hillary's last screwup on their own. Besides, she has something on us, too," he added with a rascal's grin.

C.J. smiled.

"When Rico and Marisol invited us to make ourselves at home here, I'm sure they were thinking the only thing we'd heat up in their kitchen was food."

They both laughed, but Hillary's interruption and the awkward encounter that had followed had failed to douse C.J.'s ardor. "So what do we do now?" she asked with a saucy smile on her lips. "I think we both could use a cold shower."

"What about a dip in the Lopez pool instead?" Ethan suggested, moving closer to wrap C.J. in a hug.

"Sounds good, but I didn't bring a bathing suit."

"Not a problem. Marisol and Rico keep a stock of swimwear in a variety of styles and sizes in their pool house just for guests. Follow me." He took her hand, moved toward the glass door, and opened it and they stepped out onto a patio and a walkway, which led to the pool house. "Last time I was here and I took a dip with them I noticed that most of the swimwear had never been worn and still had the store tags on it."

"Talking about thinking ahead. . . ."

"Marisol is the superorganized one of the two who is always prepared. They're cool people. I want you to meet them one day. I know you'll like them."

C.J. bit her lip as uneasiness crept over her. Her plans for Ethan didn't extend to meeting his family or close friends. She'd convinced herself that all she wanted from him was something enjoyable but casual, uncomplicated, and most of all *brief*. Something that wouldn't call for much of an emotional investment. She could not afford to get too attached to any man. Just wasn't a good idea under the circumstances.

Most of the men she'd encountered jumped at a no-strings arrangement, but she was quickly discovering that Ethan was not like most men. Maybe she and Ethan really needed to talk so each could share expectations upfront. Clarify some things. But she dreaded dragging the conversation there. Wasn't it usually the woman who made the first attempt—often way too prematurely—to define a relationship? Maybe there was another way she could get her wishes across without actually being so crude as to come out and say, *"Ethan, I only want a few laughs, some good conversation, and oh yeah, your hot bod rockin' against mine."*

"Rico's been my best friend since freshman year in college," Ethan said. "He was my roommate all four years. He met Marisol at a frat party junior year and the two have been inseparable ever since." He opened the pool house door; then both stepped inside.

Ethan moved to a wicker armoirelike piece of furniture and opened it. Bathing suits for men, women, and children in a wide variety of sizes hung from the rack with tags still dangling from several of them. There was even an unopened box of disposable swim pants for babies and toddlers inside. "See, told ya. Marisol thinks of everything." He reached for a brand-new pair of black Speedo briefs and checked the tag. "Just my size."

Out of habit C.J. reached for the brown one-piece suit with the racer back and modestly scooped neckline, the most conservative cut among the women's suits. Save for the color, it looked exactly like the beige one she had at home. She lifted it from the rack.

"Oh no, no, no." Ethan furrowed his brow and pursed his lips disapprovingly. "Not that one."

"What's wrong with it?"

"If you've got it, flaunt it. And believe me, baby," he drew in a deep breath as his hooded dark eyes gleamed with obvious desire for her, "I have noticed you've got it in spades. But you seem to go out of the way to try to hide that fact under no-frills jeans and T-shirts. Here." He plucked a white string bikini from the rack and checked the tag for the size. "Now this one is way more fitting that . . . hmmm, let me guess . . ." He hooked his Speedo and the white bikini back on the rack so he could place his hands on C.J.'s waist before letting them slide slowly and sensually down to her hips, then to the back pockets of her jeans, where he slipped his hands inside and squeezed the firm curves of her rear. "Hmmmmmmm," he rasped against her cheek. His hands inched upward against her waist, then continued their ascent until his fingers skimmed the outer curves of her breasts. His thumbs moved inward and traced teasing circles around hard nipples that strained through the fabric of her bra and T-shirt. His deft touch and the hungry look in his eyes were an instant turn-on. She felt a warm surge of silky dampness between her thighs, and her limbs trembled with a yearning as powerful as what she'd felt when they were going at it in the Lopezes' kitchen.

C.J.'s eyelids grew heavy and her tongue darted out to moisten her lips. "What are you doing to me, Ethan Tanner?" she asked, her breath now short and choppy.

"Checking your measurements, of course," he whispered thickly, tipping his forehead down to touch hers.

"I could've told you what they were had you asked."

"Yeah, but you must admit, that would not have been nearly as much fun as this." Ethan's hands slipped inside the back pockets of her jeans again and he tugged her closer until she felt his hardness nudge her belly button. "Let's see, you're a thirty-six, a very nice full C, twenty-three, thirty-six. That white bikini is going to fit you perfectly."

"But . . . um . . . ," C.J. said, "I'm all for comfort over style. That bottom is too brief. Looks as if it's cut to give the wearer a colossal wedgie."

"It's not a thong."

"You mean it's not butt floss. True, but it's not far from it," she parried.

"All right, I won't push." Ethan sighed in surrender, then released her. "I do want you to be comfortable."

"You do?" His quick retreat caught C.J. off guard.

"Yeah, and if you truly feel that sexy white number is not you and that dowdy brown one is you, hey, go for it." Ethan grinned as if to show her there were no hard feelings.

"You make it sound like a full-body neoprene wet suit for deep-sea diving or something. And it's not dowdy brown. It's more like a mocha or a milk chocolate brown. It would look great against my skin."

"All right, I'm sure you'll look fetching in whatever you choose to wear—even burlap, though that might prove quite itchy."

C.J. smiled as relief rushed through her. After all, just that morning she was thinking how nice it was to meet a man who seemed to appreciate her exactly as she was—safe clothes, muscle car obsession, trucker job, and all.

"You can have this place to change in private. I'll go to the house, check on Hillary, and change." Ethan plucked the Speedo off the rack and made a move toward the door. With his hand on the knob he looked over his shoulder with a smile and a wink. "See you at the pool in ten minutes."

After Ethan closed the door behind him, C.J. took the brown one-piece suit to a free-standing mirror in the corner, then placed it in front of her and studied her reflection. "It's perfect," she said with complete confidence.

13

Ethan was finishing up his third lap in the Olympic-size in-ground pool when C.J. sashayed poolside wearing that brown suit. She'd secured her hair in a tight bun at the nape of her neck. He swam to the edge of the pool and treaded water. Full, firm breasts, tiny waist, curvy hips, and long, toned legs made the muddy brown one-piece look downright decadent, in the best kind of way, of course. Ethan whistled, then crooned, "Hmmp, hmmp, hmmp. Woman, you *are* a work of art."

C.J. giggled, dipped one foot in the pool to stir a splash in his direction. "So are you taking back what you said about how dowdy this suit is?"

"You bet I am!"

C.J. sat at the edge of the pool with her feet and legs in the water.

"What are you waiting for? Come on in." Ethan tugged at her legs.

"Gimme a second." C.J. got up and walked to the shallow end and climbed down the pool's ladder.

Ethan swam over to meet her. "You can swim, right?"

"Well . . . um, not really."

" 'Not really'? What does that mean?"

C.J. walked in until the cool water met her bust-line. The water hit Ethan at the lower half of his muscle-rippled torso.

He noticed that she was gawking at his bare chest and practically licking her lips.

"Like what you see?" he asked with a randy grin.

"Yeah, a lot," she cooed, heating the water a few degrees in the process. In seconds the pool would feel like a hot tub, but they had to be on their best behavior. The housekeeper could be watching.

He moved to a safer topic. "You never did answer my question. Can you swim?"

"Like a brick," she deadpanned. "I took swimming lessons one summer at the Y when I was a kid. Never quite got the hang of it. It didn't help that I never practiced beyond those lessons."

"But you own swimsuits—"

"I've been to pool parties and beaches. You don't actually have to get *in* the water to enjoy the water, ya know. One of my favorite things to do in the summer when I'm on the road near a coast is to get some sunscreen, a juicy mystery novel, a cold fruity drink, and take in some rays while relaxing at a beach."

"Yeah, I suppose that can be enjoyable, but you don't know what you're missing, not experiencing the water to the fullest."

C.J. made circles in the pool with both hands, then reached up to remove the band securing her bun. Her hair fell in loose waves. She slipped the band around her wrist, inhaled a deep breath, held it with her cheeks puffed out, then dipped her head in the water for a moment. She popped up, exhaling. Her hair was now wet and slicked against her head, neck, and shoulders. Crystallike droplets of water clung to her dark brows, lashes, and honey-colored skin. "I keep telling myself I will learn one day."

"It's never too late." Ethan reached for her hands. "In fact, I can give you your first crash course now if you're game."

"You sure you don't just want to enjoy this gorgeous pool? It can't be all that much fun playing teacher."

"Oh, I'm sure I'll be very entertained," he said, moving to take a position behind her. He wrapped her up in his arms. She pressed the curve of her rear against him. He bent to lower his chin to her shoulder, then softly nibbled on her earlobe.

"Teacher, you keep that up and I won't be able to hear or comprehend a word you say."

With his hands clamped to her waist he lifted her

a bit. Her beautiful brown legs floated to the water's surface. He swayed her left, then right. Ethan's swim briefs grew snug in front as his body responded to their closeness. If he was serious about making sure she actually got something useful out of his instructions he'd have to put more space between them, but when he had her in his arms it was difficult to let go.

"First, we'll start with breathing techniques; then we'll work on your strokes and kicks . . . if time allows before dinner. Sound like a plan?"

"Or I could stay in your arms . . . just like this," she countered, her voice dropping to a seductive zone. "And learn to swim some other time—maybe back home in Detroit at some indoor pool at a Y or fitness center, when the setting is not so luxurious and day isn't as perfect."

"You do have a point."

"Rain check on those lessons, okay?" C.J. turned in the circle of Ethan's embrace.

He lifted her up until their lips met, then plunged his tongue inside the warm, sweet cavern of her mouth as she encircled his neck with her arms.

They could only take things so far, though, not knowing whether Hillary was still inside the house or not.

After frolicking in the pool for an hour, they returned to the house to find Hillary still at work, so Ethan suggested that he and C.J. get cleaned up and change for dinner. The Lopezes had left a list of restaurant suggestions taped to the refrigerator in

case the pair decided they preferred to eat out. The
list had the usual Italian and high-end steak house
options, but also several selections from which they
could choose if they desired a more adventurous
culinary experience. Together they decided to ex-
periment with something neither had tried before.
There was a Malaysian restaurant on the list that included a notation from the Lopezes: *This is our favorite of the them all.* So Malaysian cuisine it was.

C.J. had packed one of her dressiest frocks—
actually, it was the only dressy frock she'd purchased
for herself in the past year. The other six she owned
were all gifts from Nina and were too hoochie in
style for C.J.'s taste.

After taking a quick hot shower, C.J. slipped into
the black crepe dress. It had a high, straight neckline,
spaghetti straps, and a hem that hovered a couple
of modest inches above her knees. Understated but
pretty, it skimmed her curves lightly. Its low scooped
back, accented with a rhinestone heart clasp, packed
just the right amount of sexy punch for C.J. The friv-
olous and flirty styling of the strappy shoes on her
feet made up for their comfort-first two-inch heels.
She'd brushed her damp hair back in a sleek, shiny
chignon that gleamed under the lights of the guest
bedroom she'd used for changing. Usually a made-
up face for C.J. meant a bit of mascara and dab of
neutral gloss on her lips. That night she'd go for
more va-va-voom, so she painted her lips, cheeks,
and eyes with complementary hues in the deep rose

family. She slipped on large dangling earrings that sparkled from her lobes as she inspected her image in a full-length mirror from the front, back, and sides. Satisfied, she reached for the little beaded black sweater that came with the dress, then draped it across one arm before adding the small satin clutch she'd placed on the bed earlier. When she moved to step outside the bedroom she found Ethan standing at the threshold poised to knock. His long, athletic frame was shown to tremendous advantage in a dark Italian suit.

"You look amazing," he said, appraising C.J. from head to toe.

She smiled, pleased that he approved of the dress, though he hadn't seen its plunging back yet. "Thank you. So do you . . . look amazing I mean."

"I was just coming to tell you our car is waiting," he said, curling one arm around her waist. In doing so, his hand grazed the skin on her back. "And what have we here?" He peeked and checked out the frock's rear view. He whistled. "Nice, very nice. A little backdoor surprise, huh?"

Ethan lifted her hand and spun her around 360 degrees, then captured her in his arms again for a quick dip that took her breath away. For a while, it seemed as if time stopped as he held her tight and they swayed to the slow melody he hummed in her ear. The wall around her heart began to crumble. He had a way of making a cynic like herself almost believe that all that hokey stuff that her twin gushed about wasn't such a bad thing after all. But C.J. reminded herself that getting too caught up in it wasn't good for her. She had to make sure that her heart wouldn't start wishing for things—like happily-ever-afters—that for her just weren't meant to be. She felt the sting of tears in her eyes and a knot of emotion formed in her throat, but she managed to keep her composure. If she was to maintain the front, she would have to withdraw from his warm embrace. She took a step away from Ethan, swallowed the lump. "We'd better get going. I'm starving," she said, trying to sound upbeat.

They said their farewells to Hillary, and Ethan left a note for the Lopezes, thanking them for the use of their lovely home. He got his and C.J.'s bags and carried them outside to the driver, who put them in the trunk. After dinner they were scheduled to return to the airport where their small plane back to Detroit awaited them.

The Chi-Town restaurant had a spectacular view of Lake Michigan, and they managed to luck up on a great corner table, though the place was practically full.

They perused the menu and their waitress graciously answered their questions about Malaysian cuisine and offered suggestions. They started with an appetizer of *roti canai* that was similar to a flaky thin pita bread, served with a scrumptious brothlike peanut sauce. A salad of shredded lettuce, shredded green papaya, baby shrimp, and lemon dressing followed.

"So what do you think so far?" Ethan asked, settling back in his seat between courses.

"It's delicious. When I get back to Detroit I'll have to do some research to see if there's a restaurant that serves Malaysian food there."

"There's got to be. Detroit is big and metropolitan enough to have at least one of everything, don't you think?"

C.J. shrugged, then dabbed at her lips with a linen napkin. "I hope you're right, but if not, I'm sure I can surf the Web and find something similar to check out during one of my road trips."

"So, tell me more about that life, the trucking thing. I'm very curious." Ethan took a sip of his wine.

"What do you want to know?" C.J. noticed the intense gleam of curiosity in his dark eyes.

"I know a woman can do anything a man does these days, but how and why did you get into it?"

"I'm not sure where to begin." C.J. drew in a deep breath. "I'll try not to bore you to death."

"Don't worry about that."

"Well, the best thing about being a trucker is the freedom. I've been a restless spirit ever since I was a little girl. I'm not stuck in some stuffy ol' office building, nor do I have some micromanaging supervisor breathing down my neck. The hours are pretty flexible. Because I own my own truck and have set up my own little business, I work only as much as I want to and I take off as much time as I want and can afford. And the biggest plus is I get to see a whole lot of this beautiful country—up close."

"Who taught you to handle a big rig?"

"When I first started I worked for a trucking company that trained all of its drivers. Once I passed exams and qualified for my commercial driver's license I was assigned a truck and given my very first load. That was about seven years ago. I didn't have to go to any special trucking school or anything like that."

"Tell me more."

"You sure?"

"Yes. I want to know you, know all about what gets the lady excited and what makes her tick." Ethan propped an elbow on the table, rested his chin in his palm.

"OK, if you insist." C.J. couldn't deny that, unlike most of her past dates, not once had Ethan acted as if he disapproved of her chosen occupation. "I haul general freight. You name it, anything from dry dog food, car batteries, to clothing. Interesting side note: If I have a load of potato chips, I have to take routes that avoid mountain passes." C.J. sipped her white wine, relishing its sweet flavor on her tongue.

"Why?"

"'Cause the bags might explode! As I discovered the hard way once. I had loose, broken chips all over my trailer."

Ethan laughed, then turned serious. His voice suddenly dipped low as if he was distracted by a troubling memory. "What about the bad weather, particularly in these parts, snow . . . ice?"

"Well . . ." C.J. paused thoughtfully. "Snow's not so bad, but ice can be scary. I've seen more than one car or truck slide, then go greasy side up."

"Greasy side up?"

"Flip over," she continued. "But since I drive year-round it can't be avoided. Haven't had any accidents yet. So far the worst thing about driving in winter weather is getting out of the warm truck for motion lotion—" Before he could ask, she caught herself and provided the translation. "Motion lotion as in fuel, not something used for sex, so get your head out of the gutter," she teased.

Ethan laughed. "I wouldn't think fueling up would be such a big deal. I mean, it only takes a few minutes, right?"

"At some of the more modern stops yes, at some places no. We're talking about fueling up a big rig, which requires anywhere from one hundred and fifty to two hundred gallons of diesel at a time. Now imagine standing out in subzero temperatures for up to a half hour to do that."

"What about safety issues? I mean, as far as being on the road all alone so often and then dealing with men at truck stops?"

"I'm not going to lie and pretend I haven't experienced a few sticky situations, but I've always handled myself just fine. Mama didn't raise a fool. There are a few male truckers who have acted resentful toward me because they think a woman's place is anywhere but behind the wheel of a rig. I have shown up at jobs and at truck stops where some will cut their eyes at me and give me the ol' chilly what's-*she*-doing-here? look."

"And that's all? Just cold looks? I would think a woman as beautiful as you are would have to deal with a lot more, you know, sexual harassment sorta issues, as well."

"I've had men trying to pick me up at truck stops if that's what you mean, but that doesn't only happen on the road. I handle it the same way I would if a man I'm not interested in tried to flirt with me in a grocery store parking lot or when I'm out at Kensington Park alone for a jog. I know Krav Maga."

"Krav Ma-what? Sounds like something we might order from the menu here."

C.J. laughed. "Krav Maga. It's a type of self-defense system that involves a lot of hand-to-hand combat. But it can be used against armed attackers as well. Branches of the Israeli military use it."

"Whoa, I'm impressed."

"So I always have options, I also carry pepper spray and a very sharp switchblade on me," she said with aplomb, just before popping another bite of her heavenly appetizer inside her mouth.

The thick brows on Ethan's face hitched high. "Switchblade?"

"Don't worry. For the record, I didn't feel the need to pack it for our little trip," she assured him with a grin. "I know bad things happen. In fact, I know of another female trucker who has suffered at the hands of some pervert. Fortunately, that hasn't happened to me, so I haven't had to resort to using the Krav Maga or my weapons yet." C.J. stopped short of explaining that when a person survived not one but two rounds of the Big C it changed his or her perception of life and mortality. They were having such a good time she didn't want to send the mood crashing by revealing to Ethan that she was a cancer survivor. Not yet anyway. She liked the way he engaged her now and she wanted it to continue. People changed the way they treated her after learning about the cancer thing.

Also, in the back of her mind she didn't expect to live to be a ripe old age anyway. She didn't even expect to see middle age. She just felt it in her gut, and as morbid and fatalistic as it sounded, she'd already accepted that as her truth.

"There are lady cops and firefighters who take bigger risks each day," she added.

"Yeah, but—"

"I know. I know. Their causes might be more palatable to folks who reason that they're risking their lives for the safety of humankind and all. Me? I'm putting myself out on the road all alone and for what? For exploding bags of potato chips," C.J. said with a self-deprecating chuckle. "Oh, wait. I almost forgot about the time I had to haul a load of cadavers for a medical school—on packs of ice, of course.

Now that might qualify as one of the loftier ways I've contributed to society."

"You don't have anything to prove, ya know," Ethan said.

A lull followed because C.J. suddenly became uncomfortable with having the focus on her. She was grateful when their server returned with their main entrées: *udang kelapa*—jumbo shrimp fried with a crispy coconut-flavored coating and *ayam rendang,* a chicken dish seasoned with red curry sauce. On the side they had bowls of coconut rice and brown rice.

"That looks and smells great!" C.J. inhaled the aromas and tried to change the subject.

Ethan reached for his fork and waited for their server to depart before shoving a chunk of juicy chicken inside his mouth. "As long as you're happy with what you do, but I imagine that life can be difficult when it comes to maintaining long-term romantic relationships."

"Who says I want a long-term romantic relationship?" C.J.'s tone was casual. She decided it was time to let Ethan know that she did not have any happily-ever-after designs on him. She just wanted no-strings fun and hoped he was open to such an arrangement.

Ethan stopped mid-chew and just stared at her. "You don't want to be in a committed relationship?"

"Not particularly." C.J. said, then filled her fork with rice and shoved it inside her mouth. "This is so good. Pass the salt, please."

Ethan's brows nearly collided and his forehead pleated as if he was confused and disappointed.

"Is there a problem?" C.J. asked.

"It's just that . . . well, I hadn't pegged you for the type."

"I'm just not all that interested in something serious and long-term." She shook her head. "Not for me. I'm sure a man as successful and handsome as yourself gets a ton of attention from women. You're not settled down yet for a reason."

"It's not about how much attention I get from women. I have a preference for real relationships. I'm into quality over quantity. And I haven't knowingly hooked up with anybody I thought was just in it for the fun. I left those days behind in college."

"Is that right?" C.J. tasted her wine to stifle a sigh of disillusionment. "Then why aren't you married?"

"I was married," he replied. He looked her straight in the eye but didn't say more.

"Oh." C.J. chose not to interrogate him. Maybe there'd been a nasty divorce that he didn't want to elaborate on right then. She could understand that, but back to the problem at hand. *Damn. Wouldn't you know it?* Players and commitment-phobic Lotharios ran rampant in Detroit's singles circles, but Ethan was one of the few guys who'd have a problem with casual relationships.

Ethan's voice shifted low with concern. "So what was his name?"

"Excuse me?"

"His name? The guy who broke your heart and made you stop believing in and wanting love."

One of C.J.'s hands rested on the table and he reached and covered it with one of his own.

"There was no *he*," she said. "The simple truth is I've never been in love, Ethan."

"So if you've never been in love how can you say it's not for you?"

"Let's not talk about anything too deep right now. Can we just enjoy each other and this delicious meal?" C.J. moved her hand away from his.

Ethan didn't appear to take offense. "I'm sorry if I got pushy again, but I meant what I said about wanting to get to know you better, C.J."

"Can we start with something easy, like my favorite colors, foods, and music? I'm having such a good time. Let's not ruin it by making things too heavy too soon."

"Fine." Ethan managed a smile.

"Thank you."

"I already know you can't swim a lick. And you loathe girlie-girl clothes."

"I don't loathe all girlie-girl clothes."

"Tonight's little black dress being the exception, of course."

"Every now and then I do enjoy showing off the softer side of C.J." She grinned. "But I'm not one of those women who are slaves to fashion or willing to risk getting hammertoes and fallen arches just to squeeze into a ridiculously expensive superhigh-heeled pair of torture devices. That would be my sister. That girl loves her designer shoes and clothing."

"And you love old cars."

"Right."

"And you have expressed an interest in horror video games. What you haven't told me that I'm dying to know is what 'C.J.' stands for."

"That's an easy one, too. Christina Joanne, but don't you dare start calling me that."

"That's a lovely name."

"Too *lovely* for a girl who loved to roughhouse and tussle with the neighborhood boys, climb trees, play with dead bugs. 'Christina' just didn't feel like a good fit, so at age six I started insisting that people call me C.J. It was 'C.J.' or I wouldn't answer. And the nickname finally stuck, much to my delight and my prissy mother's chagrin. Eventually she relented and started calling me that, too. Her plan had been for me and my twin Nina to have girlie rhyming names and frilly pastel dresses with matching bows. Nina loved the stuff, but I wasn't having any parts of any of that."

"A real tomboy."

"I'll always be. At least now I can tolerate skirts, dresses, and even pantyhose if the occasion calls for them. But back in grade school, if Mom tried to make me wear a dress, I used to pack an extra pair of pants and a shirt in my satchel and change after I got to school. In the wintertime I'd just wear the pants and shirts under my skirts and dresses. I'd roll my pant legs up so Mom couldn't see them when I left the house. Fortunately, Nina never ratted me out."

"Tell me more about your twin."

"A lot of people think we're identical because we look so much alike, but we're fraternal."

"Having a twin must be very cool. I always wanted a twin, or any other sibling, for that matter. I was an only child. My grandmother—we called her Gran— who passed away when I was twenty, and Gus raised me."

"What happened to your parents?"

"My mother and father were never married," Ethan revealed. "Seems they just had some hot times together and then they had an *accident*. That would be me. My mother, Charmaine, a true party girl, I'm told, knew her limitations. She turned over full custody to my father, Robert, then took off. Never heard from her again. Dad did the best he could, but then war called and he had to do his duty for his country. He had to leave me with his father. That would be Gus. Dad never returned from Vietnam alive. Died in combat."

"I'm sorry to hear that," C.J. said in a low voice as she reached out to touch his hand in a sympathetic gesture.

"It wasn't easy adjusting to all that sadness and upheaval as a boy, but Gus and Gran did the best they could. They went out of their way to make sure I wanted for nothing—including emotional support.

I always felt their deep love. True, it was screwed up, not having my parents around, but Gus and Gran were so great, I really can't complain. There are a lot of kids out there stuck with bad parents and saddled with horrible childhoods that will leave them scarred for life. I truly think I would've been worse off had I been with Charmaine, who clearly did not have a maternal bone in her irresponsible party-hearty body. I would've loved to know my father, however. He did want me, I'm told, but that just wasn't in God's plan for me, obviously."

"What a great attitude you have. Doesn't sound as if you have any issues regarding your parents."

"Don't get me wrong; it wasn't that easy. I had my days. I grieved. I hurt. I was confused and I'm ashamed to say, sometimes even suffered bouts of embarrassment that Gus and Gran were always so much older than all the other parents and guardians who showed up at various school functions. The strange looks Gran and Gus got and the questions from other kids about the whereabouts of my real parents were difficult for a little boy who just wanted to fit in and be like all the other kids. But as I grew older I realized it could've been a lot worse had I not been blessed with Gus and Gran."

"I like Gus."

"And you've would've loved Gran. She was a pistol—like you—but that's just what Gus needed." Ethan took a quick trip down memory lane. "She

was so funny and filled with love and wisdom. Are
you close to your parents?"

C.J. paused a moment too long before respond-
ing. "Um, yeah. I suppose. We have our issues, but
I know they love me and only want the best for me."

"You and Nina must be very close."

"Yeah, different as night and day, but still extremely close." A small smile curled C.J.'s lips. "I
have a great relationship with my sister. She's the
top-earning hairstylist at a very trendy upscale shop
in Bloomfield Hills. I'm very proud of her."

While they finished their meal they engaged in
more small talk until their server returned to clear
away their entrée plates and take their dessert orders. It took extra effort on Ethan's part to keep the
conversation light, but he respected C.J.'s wishes.
After all, it wasn't as if he'd been all that forthcom-
ing about his own situation. He had yet to reveal any
details about the wife and child he had lost. Opening
up to people about the tragedy and how deeply it
had affected him always made him feel so vulnera-
ble and exposed. His memories of Leigh-Ann and
Hailey were so precious to him. And he couldn't just
trust anyone with such insight to his emotions regarding those losses. But judging by the way he was
feeling about C.J. already, he knew a time would
soon come when he would want to share *everything*
with her.

Though he was disappointed when she'd revealed

she had no use for love and committed romantic relationships, he wasn't about to give up on her yet. The undeniable comfort and chemistry they felt in each other's company were difficult to ignore. Their server returned, briefly breaking through Ethan's reverie, with their dessert, a sweet coconut ice cream with buttered fried banana. C.J. would come around, Ethan thought to himself with confidence. It was just a matter of time.

14

Early the next morning the phone rang, jolting C.J. from sleep. One arm snaked from beneath a quilt to grab the receiver, knocking over a picture frame and assorted bric-a-brac on the nightstand. Keeping her head under the covers, she put the phone to her ear and answered in a sleep-muffled voice.

"Hey, Sis!" Nina's annoyingly perky greeting bounced through the phone line like a cheery Christmas carol. "Just wanted to check to make sure you got home OK. How did it go?"

"Great. We went to Chicago for the day. We flew in by small private jet."

"Ooooh, big spender. Sounds as if he's really going all out to impress you."

"But you know it doesn't take much."

"You being a woman of simple taste and all. The private jet is more my style."

C.J. finally opened her eyes, then gasped, "What the . . . !" She'd thrown the covers off her head and startled at the sight of the furry mink-brown heap stretched across her thighs. "Pryde!" C.J. screeched. Another soft white heap rested to her right, near her head, Joi. Nina's two Persian cats. C.J. had forgotten that she had promised to cat-sit the critters while Nina was away on a four-day trip to New Orleans for a hairdressers' convention.

Nina had obviously dropped the cats off at C.J.'s place sometime the night before.

When C.J. returned home from her Chi-Town excursion with Ethan, she'd been too exhausted to notice her feline houseguests were there. Adjusting to their change in locations or caught up in a deep sleep, Pryde and Joi had not come running out when C.J. stepped through the front door just before 1:00 a.m. But they had found their way to her room and made themselves quite comfortable in her bed while she slept.

"You found my fur babies!" Nina trilled. "I used my key to drop them off on my way to the airport. I want to thank you again, Sis, for agreeing to keep an eye on them while I'm in New Orleans. I feel much better now, knowing they're at your place until I get back. I worry about those two so when I have to take trips. They punish me by leaving little smelly—"

"I know," C.J. said wearily. "They poop in your best pumps and annihilate your plants when you leave them at your place all alone for longer than a day or two."

"The professional pet sitters only stay long enough to put fresh water and Cat Chow in their bowls and change their litter box."

"You've already filled me in on Pryde's and Joi's abandonment issues."

"I do appreciate your taking them in for a few days. And the timing was great. You're usually out on the road when I need a reliable sitter."

Still fighting through a sleep haze, C.J. read the nightstand clock's digital display: 10:32 a.m. She bolted upright in bed when she realized she'd slept longer than she intended. Her head swam from the abrupt motion. Aunt Ella was expecting her for brunch at 11:00 a.m. "Glad you arrived in New Orleans safely. I know it won't be all work and no play while you're there, so there's no need to tell you to have fun. I know you will."

"Yeah. Registration is all day and the seminars start tomorrow. I hope to go to the receptions, meet-and-greets, today, then see a bit of the city. I really want to check out some of the sights and the great restaurants here. Now tell me about your date with Ethan."

"I'll have to fill you in another time. I told Aunt Ella I'd come over for brunch, and I'm going to be late." C.J watched the cats rise, stretch languidly, then leap off the bed in search of food. Swiftly moving out of the covers, she swiveled her legs to the side of the bed.

"Oh, OK. We'll talk later."

When the call ended, C.J. darted another glance at the clock, then decided to call her aunt and let her know she was running late.

After buying herself some time, she fed the cats, then checked the litter box Nina had placed near the back door. C.J. then showered, dressed, and headed out the door to her pickup.

An hour and half after Nina had awakened C.J., she was sitting at Aunt Ella's kitchen table.

During their meal C.J. noticed that though her aunt tried to make small talk, it was obvious that she was distracted.

"Is something wrong? Are you feeling all right?" C.J. asked as she helped her aunt rinse the dishes and load them into the dishwasher.

"I'm sorry, C.J.; my mind was elsewhere," Ella said. "Just before you arrived, Alva called."

"That's one of the older ladies who attend your church, right?"

"Yeah, she's a fellow church member, friend, and, as of a month ago, employee down at the shop."

"She works for you now?"

"Yes. She retired but needed the extra income to make ends meet, so I hired her when I had an opening. Anyway, her son called me just before you arrived to tell me she took a nasty spill, broke her hip bone. She's going to be out of commission for a while."

"Her hip bone. That's awful."

"Tell me about it. I'm worried about her. I plan to go see her later today. But her absence has me way short on help down at the shop."

"But you still have Lorenzo, right?"

"I gave Lorenzo the OK to take the next three weeks off. He had to head down to Memphis to care for his sick mother, who just had surgery."

"Bummer, Aunt Ella. If there's anything I can do?"

"Actually, there is. It would be great if you could help me out at the shop for a few days, just until I can get a temp or something. Did you have a run scheduled?"

"I haven't committed to anything, if that's what you're asking. But I have received some calls about potential jobs; I just haven't found out the particulars—the dates and locations—just yet."

"I'm just talking a few days, less than a week, if you can swing it, honey. It would mean so much to me. Your father is too busy with his business and all. And you know how your mother feels about my shop. As hard as I've worked to run a classy, reputable company, there will always be those people who think of pawnshops as shady, scummy dives that deal in trashy, stolen, or faulty merchandise. Your mother is no exception." With a full dishwasher, Ella added cleanser, secured the door, and activated the wash cycle.

"Sorry about Mom." C.J. gave Ella a sympathetic smile, because her aunt was dead-on regarding Grace's opinion regarding the business.

Aunt Ella's husband, Claude, had opened A-One Jewelry & Loan on Evergreen Road in 1962. When Claude passed away twelve years ago Ella decided to hang on to the place, though she'd received plenty of lucrative offers for it. She'd been running the business, which was based inside a three-thousand-square-foot building in Southfield. She kept her license up-to-date, and her Better Business Record was pristine.

Ella was also selective about the wares she stocked, preferring to take on what she considered high-end, quality merchandise such as jewelry, furs, and electronics. For safety and moral reasons she did not deal in firearms.

The two women took seats at the kitchen table.

"I thought about asking Nina if she could come by a few hours after she left the beauty salon, but that child is so scattered sometimes, bless her heart. Don't tell her I said this, but she would be more of a burden than a blessing, I'm afraid."

"Don't worry. I'll be happy to help out for a few days. Shouldn't be a problem," C.J. assured her, feeling a little odd that for the first time in a long while she wasn't all that eager to take on another load so soon. She told herself that feeling had nothing to do with her rapidly growing interest in Ethan. She just needed a break—a real vacation—from that road life, that's all. Now she had a good reason to linger close to home. Aunt Ella needed her. Besides that, there was no way she could leave for a long road trip now with the Dream Cruise weekend fast approaching.

Ella had a warm smile for C.J. "Thanks, C.J. You're such a sweetheart. You've come through for me twice in less than a month."

15

So it's settled, then? We're still going with this live band, though they've yet to find a substitute lead vocalist?" Beatrice placed a sterling-silver tray with cups and pots of hot coffee and tea on the table in her formal dining room.

Ethan, Jacinda, and several of Leigh-Ann's other friends and family members huddled around the table discussing more details about the upcoming fund-raising gala.

"Yeah, they've assured us that the replacement will be equally capable and talented. I believe them. What do you think, Ethan?" Jacinda asked.

Ethan's mind had started wandering about an hour into their planning meeting.

"Ethan." Jacinda tapped his arm lightly, in an effort to coax him back into the conversation.

Ethan startled. "Huh?"

"You want to trust the band to find a suitable replacement for the lead vocalist who can't show for the gala?" Beatrice settled back in her chair at the table.

"Whatever you all think is best." Ethan just hoped his failure to contribute more ideas and opinions wasn't mistaken for total lack of interest. He wanted the gala to be a success, but he just wasn't that great with details such as table centerpieces, music, and entrée selections. He and Leigh-Ann's father had been more than willing to concede to the women on such matters.

"Great," Beatrice said, clasping her hands together. "Looks as if we're all in agreement. We'll stick with the live band we've chosen. I wasn't even sure if we could get another at this short notice anyway. I never did like disc jockeys at big, classy affairs. This gala has to be extra special and everything has to be perfect—great gourmet food, fine wines, and tuxedos."

When the meeting ended a half hour later everyone but Ethan and Jacinda had departed. Jacinda helped Beatrice with the dishes. Ethan thought it was the perfect time to broach the subject of Beatrice possibly taking over his interest in Luminesque.

"It was as if you read my mind," Beatrice said, clearly intrigued by the idea. "I didn't say anything because I wasn't sure how you two would feel about my involvement. You seem to be handling things pretty well." She sat on the living room sofa while Ethan and Jacinda took their places on a flanking love seat.

"That's the thing. See, Cinda's really been doing all the work. I haven't done much of anything, to be perfectly honest," Ethan said.

"That's not true," Jacinda demurred. "Ethan, you've been a great sounding board and have offered some valuable feedback when I've come to you with various ideas and updates."

Jacinda was definitely exaggerating his contributions, but he decided not to quibble over it. He wasn't quite sure why she seemed hell-bent on maintaining the status quo when it was obvious that Beatrice, who had expressed genuine interest, would do a better job than he would. Ethan was clearly a liability.

"So are you two thinking of bringing me in as third partner?" Beatrice asked.

"I'm thinking of backing out and offering the interest in the business that I inherited to you, Beatrice," Ethan said.

"How would you feel about that?" Beatrice looked to Jacinda.

"It would be fine," Jacinda said with a tight smile and jingly voice that sounded forced to Ethan. The almost imperceptible clenching of her teeth gave her away.

"Great! I'd love to take you two up on the offer.

I know how much Luminesque meant to Leigh-Ann, and this will be another way for me to honor her memory and carry on her vision and goals. Of course, I don't know much about the actual designing itself, but I know what looks good and I'm sure I can help you with business decisions—particularly in the areas of marketing and public relations. I'm so excited! My life had become pretty boring since retirement. Cinda, when is our first Luminesque meeting?"

Jacinda narrowed her eyes at Ethan. "I'll have to check my planner, Beatrice. I'll get back to you soon."

"Splendid!" Beatrice sprang up from her chair. "I've got to tell Stan about this! I'll be right back!"

"Well, I'd better get back to the shop." Ethan came to his feet.

Jacinda checked her watch. "I've got to get going, too. I have another meeting with a potential buyer in less than an hour."

"Oh, OK. Thanks for coming by and thanks for your input on the gala during all these weeks of planning *and* this wonderful opportunity." Beatrice went to them both and planted good-bye pecks on their cheeks before flitting excitedly from the room.

Jacinda clearly didn't appreciate Ethan initiating the Luminesque conversation with Beatrice before Jacinda had agreed to the arrangement. It had become clear to him, however, that if he waited for Jacinda to do it herself it would never happen. Still, he wanted to make an attempt to smooth things over between them.

He started, "Cinda, I—"

Jacinda gathered her purse, breezed by Ethan like a chilly wind, and refused to meet his gaze. "I really do have to go. I'm going to be late."

"You'll see this is for the best. Beatrice will be more help to you and the business."

Silently Jacinda kept moving toward the door, then closed it behind her.

Later that day Ethan drove to his flagship auto shop. It was the perfect time to catch up on some paperwork because his business was closed. There would be no interruptions from staff or customers. He aimed to get something done, but once he laid eyes on the shiny red Barracuda, he had C.J. on the brain again. He lifted the hood and checked under it thoroughly, then climbed inside the car to scrutinize the interior. He then inspected the exterior from grille to bumper, admiring what a great job Gary and the bodywork team had done. C.J. was going to be so thrilled when she saw the vehicle for the first time in its overhauled state. He smiled, thinking the damn car probably looked as good as—maybe even better than—the day it rolled off the General Motors assembly line. And it was done just in time, too. The Dream Cruise would take place the following weekend. He couldn't wait to phone C.J. He eagerly dialed her home from his office phone but got her answering machine, so he left the cryptic message:

"Hey, C.J. This is Ethan. I have news for you. Gimme a call as soon as you get a chance." He hung up, then made an effort to get some paperwork done. Because he would be turning over his interest in Luminesque to Beatrice he was eager to get started on a proposal for a collector/classic car dealership. Something he'd been wanting to pursue for a while. He'd been preparing to take the first organizing steps in that direction when he lost Leigh-Ann and Hailey. After that it was all he could do to get out of bed each day to run his existing businesses when he was in so much pain. The plan to add that new arm to his auto repair and body shop chain had fallen by the wayside. Now was the perfect time to explore that option again.

By early evening Ethan left the shop and returned home. He was disappointed that he hadn't heard from C.J., but Jacinda phoned when he stepped inside his loft. She let him have it right after he uttered "hello."

"How dare you put me on the spot like that with Beatrice!" Jacinda ripped into him.

"You knew I wanted out. I'd already given you many opportunities to buy me out, but you declined. I thought it was only fair that Beatrice took over. Her daughter co-founded the business, remember?"

Jacinda decided she'd tired of debating about that and moved on to something else. "What have you been doing?" she asked, her tone inappropriately demanding.

"Excuse me?"

"I tried to phone your cell several times and you didn't answer."

Ethan moved the receiver from his ear and just stared at it incredulously. Since when did he have to check in and log his whereabouts and activities with her? Had she lost her damn mind? She'd been stomping over the bounds of their friendship lately and he didn't like it one bit, but he would refrain from calling her on it that day. It was obvious she was still flustered and frustrated because she felt blindsided by what Ethan had done at the gala meeting.

"Are you going to be all right, Cinda?" he asked patiently.

"I don't want to get into it over the phone. May I come over? I can be there in no time."

Ethan checked his watch, then agreed to let her drop by because she sounded so upset.

When Jacinda arrived, he escorted her to the living room and served wine, hoping that would calm her frazzled nerves.

"So what's going on?" Ethan asked, relaxing in the seat adjacent to the sofa where she sat.

"I was going to discuss this with you after the gala meeting, but I was so angry at you . . . Well, I won't get into that again. Anyway, I went to an accessories trade show hoping to get more accounts for Luminesque—"

"Shouldn't you be discussing this with your *new* partner?"

"I am going to fill her in, but I think you might want to hear this first. You know how much this business meant to Leigh-Ann and—"

"All right, all right." Ethan ran one hand down his face in exasperation, but let Jacinda continue anyway. It was obviously going to take her a while to adjust to the fact that Ethan was no longer involved with Luminesque.

"While at the trade show I saw a woman there wearing Cassiopeia."

Ethan didn't have a clue. "Cassiopeia?"

"Yes. The Cassiopeia earrings were a part of a collection of ear jewelry Leigh-Ann had designed and named after the constellations."

Jacinda opened her attaché case and removed a glossy color photo and colored pencil sketch of an earring. The oversize chandelier-style earring was about the size of a credit card. It had been fashioned from sterling silver, white satin ribbon, fuchsia beads, and purple crystals, according to the notes jotted on the yellow Post-it attached to the pencil sketch.

That jogged Ethan's memory. "Oh yeah, I do remember how excited Leigh-Ann was about that collection. So you saw a woman wearing the earrings." Ethan shrugged. "That's a good thing, isn't it?"

"It would be if we had made them available to the public or sold the design rights to another company. We hadn't."

"Oh." Ethan had to take a moment to assimilate what Jacinda was trying to tell him. Someone had stolen Leigh-Ann's hard work, and Luminesque wasn't profiting from it. "Are you sure it was Leigh-Ann's work? A lot of designs look similar. Could it be a coincidence that the style—"

"No. I'm positive. Who knows Leigh-Ann's work better? Who has seen every piece she created through all the stages of development—from rough sketch to final product?"

"You."

"I got a close look at those damn earrings. It's Leigh-Ann's design, I tell you. I'm absolutely sure of it. They're either Leigh-Ann's design or precise knockoffs."

"But how?"

"Well, I asked the woman where she got the earrings and she told me she purchased them at Drew-Lange a couple of weeks before."

"Drew-Lange the department store?"

"Yup." Jacinda's eyes flashed with anger as if she was reliving the moment she'd confronted the woman. "Ethan, I tell you, this overwhelming urge to execute a snatch and dash took ahold of me."

Ethan raised his eyebrows.

"I mean, it felt like such a violation of Leigh-Ann's memory, but I managed to keep my composure, of course."

"That's good. After all, this woman was obviously unaware that she was wearing a design that had been stolen from the company, right?"

"Yeah, she said she got them from the Drew-Lange

store in Dearborn. No, wait. It could've been the store in Troy. And get this: The saleslady behind the jewelry counter there told her they were selling like hotcakes. I asked the woman what she paid for them and she scribbled down the price. I couldn't believe what they were charging. They're making a killing. Of course, we have to sniff out who the real thief is."

"*We*? As in you and Beatrice? I'm turning over my interest in the company to her, remember? Not sure if it's even my place to . . ." His words trailed off. "Wait. I'll be back in a sec." He stood, then went in search of his checkbook. When he returned he asked, "How much do you need?"

"Excuse me?"

Ethan sat down, placed the checkbook on the arm of his chair so he could write in it. "I know Luminesque is barely operating in the black, so I'm assuming you need additional financing to hire a good attorney so you can sue the pants off whoever is responsible. I know lawsuits like this against big companies with bottomless pockets can't be cheap."

"So that's it?" Jacinda looked shocked. "Aren't you outraged?"

"Of course I am. Nobody steals Leigh-Ann's hard work and gets away with it. I'm all for Luminesque fighting. I'm sure Beatrice will agree. You really need to let her in on this, too. ASAP."

"So you just write a check and that will make everything all right? That's the end of your part?"

Ethan pushed out a thick, frustrated sigh. "And

what else should I be doing, Jacinda? Anything I do or say these days that involves Leigh-Ann doesn't seem to meet your approval. What is with you?"

Jacinda wouldn't meet Ethan's questioning gaze, but he noticed that her chin trembled and her eyes filled with tears. "It's just that Leigh-Ann was so special to me—"

"And we all appreciate that, but you really need to get a grip and calm down. You're wound so tightly these days. We all loved Leigh-Ann and we miss her and Hailey, but they're gone. You have to move on or you're going to drive yourself crazy. I'm sure Leigh-Ann wouldn't want you to suffer like this."

As the tears dampened Jacinda's cheeks, Ethan's annoyance fled. He moved to take a seat next to her on the sofa. He pulled her close and curled a comforting arm around her. She held him tight and buried her face at the curve where his neck and shoulder met. He comforted her for a good half hour. When she'd composed herself she phoned Beatrice to tell her what she'd learned about the theft so far, and they made plans to meet the next day to discuss strategy on how they should proceed.

"Ethan, I'm sorry if it seems as if I've been exploding on you a lot these days," Jacinda said as Ethan escorted her to her car.

Ethan held her attaché case while she removed her keys from her purse. "Just take care of yourself." He took the keys from her hand, inserted them in the lock, opened the door, and placed her case inside while she watched.

Ethan pulled her close and placed a quick kiss on her forehead. "Pamper yourself; get a massage, facial, and pedicure. You know, those little pampering perks that women like to treat themselves to when stress gets the best of them."

Jacinda looked up at him with a sheen of tears in her eyes. "Thanks for being so understanding. I know I've behaved like a shrew the last few times we've seen each other."

"Forget about it."

Jacinda got inside her car.

"Oh, I almost forgot. My donation." Ethan reached inside his back pocket and tried to pass her a check for the legal fees that might ensue.

"No, you hang on to that until Beatrice and I figure out how we're going to proceed with this."

"I want you both to keep me posted." Ethan put the check back in his pocket, then closed her car door.

"We will."

He spoke to her through the open window. "I do care, Jacinda."

"I know you do, Ethan." She gave him a small smile as she started her engine.

16

When C.J. got home, Pryde and Joi met her at the door with an enthusiastic welcome, alternately purring and rubbing their plump, furry bodies against her ankles. She fetched dinner for them and made herself a chef's salad.

After dinner she settled in a cushy chair in the living room with the latest issue of *Popular Hot Rodding* magazine, which she'd been meaning to read for a week, and a chilled caffeine-free cola. She'd deal with the nasty aftertaste. Since she'd cut back on her caffeine consumption those annoying muscle twitches had disappeared. She didn't want them returning full force. She'd just finished an article on the Wisconsin man who won the 2005 Muscle Car of the Year award with a 1969 sea green Camaro when the cordless phone on her coffee table rang.

C.J. answered and was excited to hear Ethan's voice.

"I want to thank you again for such a wonderful time in Chicago," she said.

Pryde leaped on the chair's matching ottoman, then onto C.J.'s lap. He stretched out and draped his body over C.J.'s magazine.

"We'll have to do something like that again soon," Ethan said.

"Yeah, let's." C.J. scratched Pryde's ears and chin, eliciting contented purrs. A jealous Joi soon joined him on C.J.'s lap, so she relaxed deeper into the cushions and prepared to stroke both cats until they got their fill. Nina had the felines spoiled rotten. "So many slammin' cars, so little time."

"Speaking of cars, have I got great news for you."

"You do?"

"Yeah. I left you a message earlier. I've been champing at the bit to tell you."

"I was at my aunt Ella's most of the day and I haven't checked my phone messages yet. What's up?"

"The Barracuda. It's ready to roll, baby."

When C.J. squealed, both felines scrambled from her lap onto the floor. "When can I see it?"

"When do you want to see it?"

"Shoot! Now, if possible!" C.J. knew it was late and the place was closed, but she was talking to the owner, who not only had the keys, but also had the authority to open the shop anytime he wanted.

"Tonight? You're serious?" Ethan sounded as if her request caught him off guard, but there was still a smile in his voice.

"As a heart attack. Where are you now?"

"Well, I was at the shop earlier today trying to get some work done. I'm home now."

"So you're probably in for the night and not eager to turn around and drive right back to the shop, right?"

"For you I would. To see your face when you get your first peek at it in its revamped state is well worth the return trip on a Sunday night. How long will it take you to get to the shop?"

C.J. was already on her feet and moving toward a closet to retrieve her Doc Martens. "I'm there."

Wearing the widest smile, C.J. stood before the shiny Rallye Red Barracuda.

The car had been moved to one of the detached storage garages stationed at the rear of the vast auto repair/body shop property. Her eyes shone brightly with ecstatic tears. Her voice was thick with emotion. "Oh, Ethan. It's beautiful, absolutely beautiful."

Ethan moved close to curl an arm around her waist. She leaned into him and tore her eyes away from the car. "It's just the way I hoped it would look with the right TLC." She'd risen up on her toes and her arms circled his neck. She turned her face up to meet his. She thanked him with a soft, sweet kiss on the lips that soon turned into a heated tongue tangling that tore moans of pleasure from their throats.

When Ethan lifted C.J. off the ground she wrapped her legs around his lean, muscled torso. With them still connected at the lips he carried her to the Barracuda's hood. She rested her bottom there as they held each other tight. Soon Ethan felt C.J. tugging his shirttail from his jeans and caressing his bare back. He took that as permission to peel layers of clothing away from her as well. He yanked at the edge of her T-shirt, pulled it over her head, then tossed it aside. He admired the curves of her sexy honey-colored breasts brimming over the top of her no-frills white bra. He quickly did away with the bra, then filled his hands with her firm flesh, kneading and lifting it. He circled her caramel areolae with his thumbs until he could no longer resist tasting the erect nipples that beckoned him. He taunted and teased them until C.J. reached for the button and the zipper of his jeans. Once she had his fly open she stroked him until he felt as if he'd explode. He ground himself against her. Her thighs locked him in a viselike grip as he plunged his tongue into her mouth again.

She'd have to release him if they were going to get her jeans off and proceed. He felt the pressure of her thighs on his hips diminish, so she'd figured it out, too.

It was only after Ethan had her panties, jeans, and

boots off that he managed to think past the sex-starved fog that had clouded his brain. With much reluctance he released C.J. and took two steps away from her naked and eager body.

"What's the matter?" she asked through hot, choppy breaths. The movement of her heaving chest just made her perfect plump breasts all the more tantalizing. Her lips were moist and swollen from the kisses. The sheen of perspiration on her skin glowed. Damn, she was gorgeous, and if Ethan didn't bury himself inside of her at that moment he just knew the craving would surely kill him. But he wasn't sure if this type of intimacy was where he should go with her so soon if he ultimately wanted something of substance with her. He still had to encourage her to change her mind regarding committed relationships.

When Ethan didn't respond to C.J. right away she looked frustrated. "Ethan, don't you want me?" she asked in a creaky voice weakened by vulnerability. She bit her bottom lip, looked away from him, and crossed her arms across her breasts as if she were suddenly embarrassed as she awaited his reply.

"It's not that, sweetheart." Ethan sighed, then shook his head, not believing his own actions when he'd gone without enjoying a woman this way for so long. An incredulous chuckle escaped from him that C.J. immediately misconstrued.

Her eyes ignited and she bit out, "What kind of game are you playing? Is it funny to get a woman naked, then leave her hanging, like some . . . some I-I don't know." Abandoning her sudden modesty, C.J. threw up her hands, and her beautiful breasts were in full view again. "Like some rusted and corroded ol' crankshaft?"

Crankshaft? Only C.J. could blather something so . . . so . . . C.J. She was definitely one of a kind and he would most definitely make her his. All his. Eventually. With time and patience, but for him that was hard to come by. He wanted her heart first. He wanted her heart now and he would've preferred to know he was definitely on track to winning it before accepting the gift she was offering him, but what felt like a titanium exhaust pipe in his pants urged him on.

"We don't have protection," he replied as an explanation as to why he suddenly stopped when things had gotten so heated.

C.J.'s scowl vanished. "That's all? Really?"

"Yes," he said, caressing her cheek.

"Why didn't you just say so, then? I got that covered." C.J. slid off the car and so did her jeans that they'd used as a barrier between her warm skin and the cool metal surface of the Barracuda's hood.

She went to the shoulder bag she placed on the ground next to a tire when they'd first entered the garage. She plucked out a small packet he knew was a condom.

"See, your friend Marisol isn't the only one who's always prepared." C.J.'s lips formed a saucy smile. She was just so adorable and too damn sexy to resist,

Ethan thought as he took her in his arms again, placed her bottom on the hood of the Barracuda, and stepped into the V of her open legs. He looked deep into her eyes as he clamped one hand around the nape of her neck. The silky waves of her ponytail caressed his hand as he drew her closer to trace the outline of her lush, sweet lips with his tongue. His fingers did the same with the slick folds between her thighs. She squirmed, wriggled closer, pressing herself against fingers that only intended to tease.

"Tell me what you want," he rasped.

"You," emerged as her breathy response.

"When?" he taunted her.

"Now."

Just when she'd rock forward to increase the pressure he'd retreat, hoping to drive her to the best of erotic madness. Their lips and tongues locked again, making Ethan feel as if he wanted to swallow her whole.

When she broke the kiss and threw her head back as if lost in a daze, he suckled her breasts, but his hand continued its own sensual pursuit, stimulating her most delicate pleasure point. He took great care and used the lightest flicking motion until she gasped for air. He could no longer maintain control of his body's response to her. With his arousal jutting from his open fly, he quickly protected them with the condom. He entered her with a single slow stroke as she held on to his broad shoulders. They rocked together, with the jeans he'd peeled off her limbs earlier providing a nice, friction-free glide across the car's shiny surface. She felt so good to him.

And he to her.

Yes. This is what I needed, C.J. thought, savoring the thick hardness pumping inside and filling her up. She moved her hands from his strong shoulders down to his tight, flexing bottom, urging him to move closer and plunge deeper until the spiraling coil in her belly descended and morphed into the most gratifying melting and pulsing sensations between her legs. She whimpered, then mewled as Ethan increased his tempo, hurling her into a rippling orgasm. She shuddered with pleasure. Ethan's thrusts grew more vigorous and powerful as he moaned against her neck, where he made tiny bites. The sound and feel of Ethan taking such undeniable pleasure in her body— a body that had betrayed her and damaged her spirit on more than one occasion—was enough to reignite her passion and set her on the path toward yet another release. She came again—only softer and gentler the second time. When the muscles in his back flexed, his body went still and she knew he was riding out his climax. And she could hardly wait for him to do it again—maybe *inside* the Barracuda the next time, she thought as she felt the weight of his hard body relax against hers. He kissed her forehead and asked, "How are you doin'? You're not too uncomfortable, are you?"

"No complaints at all, but I was sorta wondering about that backseat."

"What about it?" Ethan's expression turned serious as he drew himself up off C.J. "Is there a problem? 'Cause if there is, I'll get the fellas on it first thing in the morning."

"I'd much prefer *you* got on it . . . like right now," she said with an impish grin that instantly gave him a clue.

"Hmmm, might be too snug of a fit," he said, taking her in his arms to lift her off the hood. She wrapped her legs around him again. "Me and you in the backseat of a two-door? In case you haven't noticed, I am not a short man, darlin'."

She kissed the tip of his nose. "True, but part of the fun will be experimenting to see how many creative positions we can come up with, don't you think?"

Ethan opened the right car door. "You have a point. I say we live dangerously tonight and worry about those chiropractic bills tomorrow."

Ethan and C.J. enjoyed each other just as much inside the car as they had outside of the car. Both lost track of time. It was a little after 11:00 p.m. when they gathered their discarded clothes and attempted to get dressed again. "Man! I swear I'm never going to look at this place the same way again." Ethan slid one long, muscle-etched leg inside his jeans, then slid in the other.

C.J. tucked her T-shirt inside her jeans. "This garage, you mean?"

"Yeah." He leaned against the car to slip on his Nikes.

"And oh, what a way to break in my 'Cuda." C.J. massaged her nape. "But I must admit the neck's feeling a little stiff now."

Ethan smirked as he laced up his athletic shoes. "Told you."

"But us jamming back there was well worth it when we were pleasantly distracted, don't you think? You had all the right moves, ya know."

Now flattered and fully dressed, Ethan went to gather her in his arms and kiss her cheek. "Why, thank you, but we shouldn't attempt some of that stuff again. I don't think my back or knees can take it. You, on the other hand, my dear, are freakishly double-jointed."

"Are you complaining?"

"Hell, no!"

"Hey, what's in the other three compartments of this garage unit?"

"I keep the International here because I live in a loft space. The building doesn't have a whole lot of secured, covered parking. And there's no way I'm going to subject my classic car collection to the elements."

"Collection? You own other old vehicles, besides that custom truck I saw yesterday?"

"Yup. The other two are here."

"May I see them?"

"Sure."

Ethan reached for a remote control unit on a nearby shelf, then took C.J. by the hand, pressed a button on the unit that raised their compartment's door. He led her to the other compartments to show off his red 1971 Corvette coupe and his yellow 1968 Chevy Impala convertible.

"These are slammin'!" C.J.'s hands flew to her cheeks.

"And I plan to acquire even more, but not just for my personal collection. I'm thinking of adding a classic car dealership to my company."

"Oh, Ethan! Really? That's so cool. You're so lucky. I'd considered going into a similar business, but I just didn't have the capital or the collateral to get the kind of financial backing I'd need to acquire the fleet of vehicles required to get started. I barely managed to purchase my own rig. You're going to do great. I'm so happy for you."

And it showed. It was that look on her face that gave Ethan an idea. One he hadn't given much thought to before blurting out, "Hey, why don't we do this thing together?"

"But I wouldn't be an equal partner because I don't have your big moneybags or boundless credit line."

"Don't worry about the money, at least not right away."

"But I don't take handouts and this is huge."

"We can work out some sort of plan or contract in which you get to invest more financially in the business and acquire a bigger slice of it as you're able. In the meantime, you can make major contributions to the business in other ways. Contributions that will factor heavily into whether the business is a success or not. You can even oversee the day-to-day operations if you want. I'm going to have to hire someone to do that anyway. I can't because I have my hands full already with the chain of auto repair and body shops. I think your genuine love for old cars, your vast knowledge, and the fact that we obviously get along would make you the perfect business partner.

"Day-to-day operations?" C.J. furrowed her brow. "Ethan, I have a job already, remember? I'm on the road most of the time."

"But for how long? Is that something you want to continue doing for years to come? Don't you think the time will come when you'll want to do something else you enjoy that would afford you the opportunity to stay closer to home more often?"

"Maybe," she said glumly. "But I'm not sure that time is now."

Ethan regretted that he'd stolen the light in her eyes. "Hey, I'm not going to push." He massaged her arms. "Seems as if I keep saying that, don't I?"

"Yes."

"But just give it some thought." Eager to get her smiling again, he moved on to a subject sure to lighten the mood. "Hey, how would you like to drive the Barracuda home tonight?"

"But my pickup—"

"You can leave it here and I'll have Monty and one of the other fellas drop it off at your house first thing tomorrow morning."

"But the office isn't open to settle my bill."

"I'm sure you're good for it. You are in tight with the owner of this place, remember? And besides, I know where you live." He winked.

C.J. beamed again. "I finally get to slip behind the wheel and hear the rumble of the engine!"

"Like the sound of a baby's first cry to a new mom."

They made their way back to the garage where the Barracuda was parked.

Ethan took the keys out of the pocket of his jeans. He opened her hand, kissed her palm, placed the keys inside, then curled her fingers around them. "It's all yours, baby."

Obviously giddy with anticipation, C.J. yanked the door and slipped in on the driver's side, jabbed the key in the ignition, and started the engine. As C.J. had ordered when relaying detailed preferences to Gary, the head mechanic, it released a deep roar that would rival Godzilla's. "No wimpy muffler system here! Woooo-hooooo!" She waved one fist in the air triumphantly. "They make more modern cars sound like gutless golf carts!" she shouted over the roar as she gave the car more gas. "I think it's akin to castrating a car!"

"Well, you know there *is* that issue of noise pollution," Ethan shouted over the noise. "That's actually important to *some* people, you know. What's music to your ears others will find inappropriate and obnoxious."

Being the auto purist that she was, C.J. flapped her hand at him dismissively. "Oh, noise pollution smoise smollution," she shouted back. "This is a real sho-nuff engine, unrestrained and free! As it should be!"

"And your neighbors are gonna love you," Ethan added with a chuckle, heavy on the playful sarcasm. Watching her so happy pleased him.

Though C.J. trash-talked about the loud engine, he knew she was not serious about shattering her neighborhood's tranquility regularly. The Dakota pickup was her usual mode of transportation while in town. The Barracuda was mostly for show. And for lavishing with her love and attention. She'd already told him she only planned to take the Barracuda out on the road for local auto shows and other special occasions such as the Dream Cruise.

C.J. eventually cut the engine and climbed out of the car. "So are you going to participate in the Cruise this year?"

"Yeah, I'm driving the International, but I can only do Friday night. There's a big—" Ethan's words dropped off. The fund-raising gala for that scholarship fund was Saturday. There was no way he'd miss that. He'd considered asking C.J. to join him, but two things held him back. He assumed her weekend nights would be booked up with the Cruise. But he also wasn't sure if it was appropriate to flaunt his romantic interest in front of Leigh-Ann's family and friends right now. And an event that was specifically held in Leigh-Ann's memory, too? What was the protocol on situations like that?

"There's a big what?" C.J. prodded.

Ethan didn't know whether he was ready to reveal that he was a widower, too. Telling her about the gala would require filling in all the details about Leigh-Ann and Hailey. He didn't want to talk about them right now but vowed to do so soon.

"Got plans I can't get out of Saturday night," he replied cryptically.

C.J. didn't seem bothered by his hesitance to elaborate. "While lots of people show up on Friday, Saturday is really the official night."

"I know."

"I'll bet that International gets lots of attention even on Friday."

"And your 'Cuda, too."

"Yeah. I can't wait."

"Is anyone riding with you?"

"Nina and Aunt Ella on Friday night. And my parents on Saturday. Are you bringing anyone along?"

"Gus. He'd love to see Ella. We should pick a place to meet and trail each other along the cruise route Friday night."

C.J. smiled. "I'd like that."

17

I still can't believe it. It looks as if everything is going to work out just fine . . . and so quickly, too. Blows my mind." Ethan relaxed on the sofa in the Whitmore living room. Following a quick meeting about Saturday's scholarship gala, Jacinda and Beatrice gave him an update on Luminesque.

"Looks as if we'll get very little resistance from those suits over at the Drew-Lange department stores," Beatrice said.

Just a few days ago Jacinda had been in a tailspin about the theft of Leigh-Ann's designs. After Beatrice and Stan got wind of it they'd put their attorney on it. He was pretty sure a huge financial settlement from Luminesque was pending.

"That was so awful, that company stealing my

baby's designs, then distributing and profiting off them," Beatrice huffed as she refilled everyone's cups with hot tea. "When Jacinda told me about it, Stan and I knew we had to do something immediately."

Jacinda took a sip from her cup. "I'm still in shock. A type of happy shock, of course. Beatrice really took over the reins on this and we came up winners!"

Ethan knew he'd been right when he advised Jacinda to extend a partnership to Beatrice, whose smarts and emotional connection to the company would make her indispensable.

"I thought we had a strong case, but I still wasn't sure that things could get settled so expeditiously," Jacinda said. "Companies the size of Drew-Lange have been known to draw out all legal battles against the little guy, who simply can't afford to continue to pursue their lawsuits for the long haul."

"Tell me about it," Beatrice cut in. "To put it bluntly, often the big company's lawyers can eat an independent designer's lawyer for breakfast. Just dragging out any suit makes it very cost-ineffective for the little guy to continue to pursue it. Think about it. Like our attorney said, we were probably talking an intellectual-property lawsuit that adds up to less than a million dollars. Our attorney's fees and costs would probably average . . . oh, let's say five hundred thousand dollars. Shoot, fees for the plaintiff could go as high as one million dollars if we had a really long fight on our hands. The bottom line is most small businesses and independent designers simply can't afford to take on the big company if it chooses to call their bluff."

"But they won't," Ethan said. "Why? That's very strange."

"They won't because of the rock solid evidence against them that we discovered."

"When you say 'rock solid evidence' you mean the dated sketches and photos of Leigh-Ann's work, right?"

"Yes. The design had been registered. It has a copyright in the U.S. Copyright Office," Jacinda added, exchanging conspiratorial grins with Beatrice. "But turns out there was even more damning evidence, thanks to Leigh-Ann."

"Oh?" Ethan was anxious to hear more.

"Seems Drew-Lange, um, made a mold of Leigh-Ann's original earrings to produce their own. And those originals included an index finger print."

"An index finger print?" Ethan echoed.

"Yes, that's right. Leigh-Ann's index fingerprint, and it has been reproduced on all the Drew-Lange rip-off earrings."

"Of all the boneheaded . . . !" Ethan threw his head back as his booming laughter rocketed around the room. "You're kidding me, right? Tell me you're kidding me. Nobody at Drew-Lange noticed this fingerprint?"

"Guess not." Jacinda and Beatrice joined in the laughter. "It was a security idea that Leigh-Ann had come up with and I found her notes on it in the Cassiopeia file. I just know Leigh-Ann is looking down on us smiling and going, 'Take that, Drew-Lange!' 'Cause she got the last laugh."

Beatrice added, "But even if we didn't have that bombshell, we were prepared to fight this one to the bitter end for Leigh-Ann. I couldn't live with myself if I didn't."

"Me, either," Jacinda seconded.

Beatrice smiled at her fondly. It was a look Ethan had noticed Beatrice often gave Leigh-Ann. It was obvious that Beatrice's relationship with Jacinda had deepened in the past few months. It was as if Jacinda had become like a surrogate daughter for her.

"Besides, we had a Plan B in the works if the legal fees had become too much to handle," Beatrice continued. "I did a lot of research on this. If the suits who ran Drew-Lange had chosen to fight us on this or tried to drag out the legal proceedings, I was going to approach the chairman and general counsel of the Made in the USA Foundation."

"What's that?" Ethan asked.

"A nonprofit Bethesda, Maryland–based organization," Jacinda replied. "It created American Crafts Project, which represents artists and craftspeople by filing intellectual-property lawsuits in federal court against big retailers for them. And check this out: It does this work pro bono."

"They were going to be our next step. If the Drew-Lange check clears and they don't breach any part of the new vendor's contract for Cassiopeia and those other two designs they managed to get their hands on, what started off as an unfortunate fiasco could turn into a match made in heaven," Jacinda announced in a jingly voice.

"Did you ever figure out how Drew-Lange got the earrings in the first place?" Ethan asked. "There's no way *you* could've forgotten something like sending samples or sketches out for that company's consideration."

"No, but apparently Leigh-Ann did just days before she died. And she didn't get around to mentioning it to me because the accident . . ." Jacinda's words dropped off.

Beatrice moved to comfort her. She sat on the arm of Jacinda's chair and gave her a hug. "Now, now. No need for tears. It all worked out," Beatrice said, patting Jacinda's back. "Let's concentrate on the positive things, right now. We'll have a humongous settlement from Drew-Lange coming!"

"Yes, you're right." Jacinda sniffled.

"And we've agreed to donate some of it to the scholarship fund and we have the gala that's just a day away. So who is your date?" Beatrice asked, playing with Jacinda's curls.

"I don't have one." Jacinda reached for a napkin on the coffee table. She dabbed at her eyes, then blew her nose with it.

Beatrice turned to Ethan. "And what about you?"

"Me what?"

"Are you bringing a date?"

"Well, I . . . um . . . ," Ethan stammered. This conversation had taken an awkward hairpin curve. But hadn't he committed to moving on with his life? Yes. But he just hadn't expected his former mother-in-law to quiz him about his dating status—especially for the gala.

Before he could reply, Beatrice added, "I was thinking . . . well . . . maybe, you could escort Jacinda. That is, if you don't have other plans. Do you? Have someone else in mind, I mean?" Beatrice asked.

"N-no!" Ethan said way too quickly, like someone with a reason to feel guilty for even considering squiring someone to a gala. "I mean, I haven't asked anyone else to join me for that evening." He thought about C.J. and how much he would've loved to invite her. He told himself there was nothing wrong with feeling that way. But was this the time to tell Beatrice and Jacinda he'd met another extraordinary woman who had him thoroughly enraptured? He decided it was not. While C.J. had made it clear how she felt about committed relationships, Ethan was still determined to change her mind. Once that was accomplished, he'd have to share that part of his life with Beatrice, Stan, and Jacinda, but he would do that only on a need-to-know basis. And with C.J.'s Dream Cruise plans and all, she wasn't available to attend Saturday night's gala anyway, so they didn't need to know about her. *Yet.*

"Then you'll be Jacinda's escort for the evening?" Beatrice asked.

"Sure. No problem," Ethan replied.

Ethan forced a grin though he felt ill at ease all of a sudden. He told himself escorting Jacinda, who was just a friend, wouldn't be like a *real date* but more like the time when he was seventeen and had agreed to accompany Cammy-Jo Foster, his pastor's daughter, to her prom. Cammy-Jo's boyfriend had bailed on her at the last minute, leaving her stuck with a nonrefundable limo rental and an expensive powder blue evening gown she'd taken an after-school job at Burger King to purchase.

"So what time are you picking her up?" Beatrice asked.

"Who?" Ethan's mind had wandered.

"Jacinda!" Beatrice replied.

"What works for you, Jacinda?" Ethan asked.

"I suppose, um . . . we could negotiate that as we get closer to the event," Jacinda replied, looking as uneasy as he felt.

However, Ethan noticed that Beatrice had watched the exchange with an odd yet satisfied expression on her face.

18

Inside A-One Jewelry & Loan, C.J. stood behind a panel of Plexiglas and tended to a customer who had brought in a billowy mink coat to pawn.

The woman had bundled it up and placed it through the revolving door cut in the safety barrier on the counter, which separated the shop workers and customers.

C.J. didn't know anything about furs and found the ostentatious ones offensive, so she called out to her aunt, who was in her office watching her printer spit out fingerprint labels. Michigan's ordinances for pawnshops required shop owners to mail fingerprints to every customer's city or town.

Ella pursed her lips as she inspected the mink,

running her fingers through the silky fur and checking the black satiny lining for damage.

"It's authentic," said the woman who brought in the coat. "And in great shape, too."

"I can see that," Ella said, not taking her eyes off the garment. She placed the coat on the counter and scribbled an offer for it on a slip of paper. She shoved the paper through another small revolving door in the Plexiglas.

"I'll take it. Also, while I'm here, I might as well give you this." The woman looked down at the sparkling marquis-cut diamond on her left ring finger and tugged it off.

"An engagement ring?" Ella asked.

The woman nodded and swallowed as if enunciating was too painful. Tears were in her blue eyes as she placed the ring inside the window and shoved it on Ella's side.

C.J. noticed the sympathetic expression on her aunt's face as she slowly reached for the jeweler's loupe in a drawer next to the glass jewelry display counter.

"You sure?" Ella asked.

The woman nodded again and encouraged Ella to get on with business. It was as if the woman believed hesitation would be too much temptation. She'd surely change her mind. "I must. My husband lost his job a few months ago. And things have gotten really bad," she explained.

Ella checked the ring and jotted down an offer.

The woman accepted it with a nod. After that business transaction was concluded and the woman had departed, C.J. just looked at her aunt, whose thoughts seemed to have left the store with the woman who'd just pawned her mink and engagement ring.

"It never gets easier, does it?" C.J. patted Ella's back.

Ella sighed. "No, not really. It's just business. But sometimes I feel like a vulture."

"You're helping people who need cash quickly and have no other options. And besides, it's not as if you're lowballing them with your offers. I've seen what you pay for some of the items, and even I know when people are as desperate as some of the ones I've seen come in here, you could get away with taking advantage and putting the screws to them, but you haven't."

C.J. was also aware that while under Michigan law shops must keep pawned goods for at least ninety days before they can be sold, her aunt would often hang on to things with obvious great sentimental value to her special customers such as engagement, wedding, and family heirloom jewelry for an additional sixty days before putting them up for sale. This provided some customers extra time to buy back their irreplaceable keepsakes and pay the 3 percent interest per month that the items had accrued in the store.

To shake off her melancholy mood, Ella suddenly piped up, "So, you all excited to take the

Barracuda out tonight? We're going to have so much fun!"

"You betcha!" C.J. checked her watch. "Ethan and Gus should be here any minute now."

Gus and Ethan had agreed to meet them at the shop and then head over to Dream Cruise central. Nina, who'd decided to extend her stay in New Orleans by several days, would not be joining them as originally planned. C.J. was a little disappointed but not angry. The Dream Cruise really wasn't Nina's thing.

The bell mounted at the top of the front door jingled, signaling that someone had entered the shop.

"Well, if it isn't two of the most gorgeous ladies in the state of Michigan," Gus bellowed as he approached the counter where C.J. and Ella stood.

"State of Michigan?" Ethan was right on Gus's heels. "I'd extend the net much wider than that. We're talking world-class beauty here, Granddad!"

Both women stepped beyond the Plexiglas barrier.

"Don't you just love those Tanner men?" Aunt Ella sang upon getting her first glimpse of Gus.

Ethan wore black jeans that flattered his muscular thighs and the blue pullover shirt that accentuated his broad shoulders and sculpted chest. C.J.'s heart did a little somersault. Her skin simmered when the images of her and Ethan naked on the hood and in the backseat of her Barracuda came to mind. This had happened at least a million times since she left his shop that passionate Sunday night.

"We were just getting ready to close up shop," C.J. said, joining Ethan and his uncle.

Gus kissed C.J. on the cheek, then passed her to Ethan, who treated her to a big hug and even bigger kiss.

Aunt Ella and Gus bussed more discreetly and linked arms.

"C.J. tells me you're driving an ol' International tonight, Ethan." Ella moved to tidy up some papers on the outer counter.

"Yeah. I call her Betsy Blue."

C.J. helped with the closing procedures and fifteen minutes later Ella was turning off the shop's light and locking the door.

Out in the A-One lot, Ethan had parked his International next to C.J.'s Barracuda. Both got inside their respective vehicles.

C.J. noted that her aunt seemed reluctant to part with Gus as she climbed into the Barracuda's passenger seat, while Gus acted as if Betsy Blue was the last place he wanted to be.

Ethan, who had started his engine, noticed as well. He smirked and shook his head, then killed the engine. "Hey, I have an idea. Granddad, you take Betsy Blue and drive her. Ella can join you. And I'll ride with C.J. in the Barracuda, if that's OK with C.J. and Ella."

Gus's and Ella's eyes flashed with obvious delight at Ethan's suggestion.

C.J. knew how much that truck meant to Ethan and had to speak up even if Gus and Ella wouldn't. "Don't *you* want to be the one to show off *your* Betsy Blue?"

"She gets her chance to shine regardless of who's behind the wheel," Ethan replied. "And I trust Granddad to treat her right. Besides, I drove her in the Cruise last year."

C.J. noticed that Gus and Ella still refrained from verbally swaying things one way or another, but the expressions on their faces clearly revealed how they wanted the four to pair off: C.J. and Ethan. Gus and Ella.

"You sure you're OK with this, Ethan?" Gus asked as a token gesture.

"Of course. I wouldn't have suggested it if it wasn't OK." He looked at C.J. "Besides, I want to spend as much time with you as I can before you take off again."

"OK, it's you, me, and the 'Cuda, then." As soon as C.J. surrendered to the new arrangement Gus hopped out of the truck and dashed to Ella's side of C.J.'s car. He looked as if he was going to attempt to scoop her out and carry her over to the truck, but Ella's warning expression gave him pause.

"Do we really want to test that bad back you told me about this way, Pookie Bear? I can think of more fun ways for you to throw your back out."

When Ella winked brazenly, C.J.'s jaw dropped.

"Yes, I suppose you're right, Apple Dumpling," Gus added.

Pookie Bear and Apple Dumpling? Spicy innuendo about backs getting thrown out? Aunt Ella had been having the time of her life with Gus and she deserved it. *You go, Aunt Ella!* C.J. thought as she and Ethan burst into laughter.

Ella pulled herself out of the car. She and Gus linked arms and chattered excitedly as they moved toward the truck.

C.J. and Ethan watched Ella and Gus scramble inside his truck like two teenagers who just had gotten their weekly allowance and permission to use the family sedan for the night.

Ethan tossed the keys to the truck to his uncle, then folded his long legs inside C.J.'s car. "Looks as if you're stuck with me." He grinned. "Ready to roll?"

"More than ready!" C.J. smiled. She then turned the ignition and her beloved Godzilla engine roared to life.

C.J.'s opportunity to show off her car was everything she'd hoped it would be. It was a warm, beautiful night with clear skies, save for the abundance of stars. Though the official Dream Cruise wouldn't take place until Saturday, the ambience of that Friday night was just as electric as crowds descended on Woodward Avenue en masse. Spectators staked out prime spots along the official Cruise route to cheer on Cruisers and admire the caravan of classic cars.

C.J. and Ethan had rolled down the windows, so a nice breeze kept them both comfortable.

Ethan watched a beaming C.J. and took great satisfaction in knowing that he'd played a part in putting that smile there by ensuring that the car had been ready in time. "Happy, huh?"

"Very!" she replied. "I'll always be grateful to you and the fellas at the shop."

Gus and Ella rode alongside them in Ethan's International. A few minutes later Gus had something he wanted to say, but neither C.J. nor Ethan could hear over the loud rumble of the Barracuda's engine. Gus honked and waved at them to signal that he was about to pull over on one of the side streets.

"Gus wants us to pull over with him," Ethan said.

C.J. changed lanes smoothly and trailed Gus along one of the cross streets. He drove into the parking lot of a CVS Drug Store. Ethan and C.J. climbed out of the car and met Gus and Ella halfway.

"What's up?" Ethan asked his grandfather.

"Ella and I were thinking it would be kinda nice to take a little romantic walk down by the river later," Gus said.

"By 'romantic' you mean just the *two* of you, huh?" C.J. clarified.

"And you need to know if I can stand to have my truck out of my sight that long, right?" Ethan asked.

"Yes." Gus drew Ella closer and kissed her cheek.

"I don't mind. You two have fun, but be gentle with Betsy," Ethan said.

"Thanks!" Ella moved out of Gus's embrace and hugged Ethan. "You know, you're not so bad for a mechanic."

Ethan found that last comment bewildering. "You got something against mechanics?"

C.J. chuckled. "I'll explain later."

Ella continued, "I know we old folks are just messing up the plan, but you two have been real good sports about it. We'll finish the route with you two, then we'll branch off near the end and—"

"Go on and do your thing," C.J. cut in.

"You don't mind, do you, honey?"

"Of course not! We can do the foursome thing some other time."

Soon Gus and Ella were back in the truck headed back to Woodward Avenue with C.J. and Ethan trailing them.

"You're not disappointed that we're not doing the foursome thing later, are you?" Ethan asked, wondering if C.J. had just put on her cheery, cooperative front for her aunt and his grandfather.

"No, not at all. I completely understand those two wanting to be alone."

"Hey, what did your aunt mean about that mechanic crack?"

"She's had a hard time with some of the shadier ones overcharging her in the past."

"Well, those days are over. You tell her to bring her car to one of my shops—I have a dozen citywide from which to choose. I'm sure she won't have a problem finding one that's conveniently located near her home or business."

"She'll be glad to hear that."

"I like Ella."

"And Gus is so funny and sweet. I'm glad that Aunt Ella has finally met someone who put the twinkle back in her eyes. I've never seen this side of her before, and it's nice."

"And what about you?" Ethan asked.

"What about me?"

"Is it just the great job my guys did on this car that put the twinkle in yours?"

"Well, if truth be told . . . I think the company I've been keeping lately has a lot to do with that."

Ethan grinned. "Glad to know that. Any ideas what you'd like to do after Gus and Ella ditch us?"

"It's such a beautiful starry night. Be a shame to let it go to waste by rushing back inside when we get to the route's end."

"We could do the route again."

"No, wait. I have a better idea. You'll see."

19

About two hours later C.J. drove into the Farelli's Grocery parking lot.

"We're grocery shopping?" Ethan asked, sounding anything but thrilled.

"No, silly!" C.J. slapped his thigh. "We're not going inside. There's something I want you to see." C.J. wheeled the car toward the back lot.

An 18-wheeler soon filled Ethan's view. C.J. parked the car next to it and announced with pride, "There she is. My home away from home."

They got out of the car and she showed off the cab and her sleeping quarters, including the mini-TV, refrigerator, laptop, and bookshelf and all the other little conveniences that made her trips more comfortable. She took out a box of kitschy souvenirs, which included postcards, shot glasses, bobble-head dolls, and giant metal belt buckles, that she'd collected from some of the cities she'd visited. Her favorite keepsake was a stuffed sock monkey she called Fu Manchu that she had picked up at a little ma-and-pa diner in Tupelo, Mississippi.

"This place is kinda homey," Ethan said of the small quarters. "All that's missing is a john."

"Of course, and as I've told you before, there are plenty of places on the road to use those and there are also places to shower," she told him.

When C.J. suggested that they climb onto the roof of the truck Ethan was reluctant, but he didn't let it show. He really did want to understand why the trucking thing was so fascinating to her.

"If we're going up there, shouldn't we try sitting on the wider, roomier trailer part?"

"We'd need a ladder, which I don't have, to get up there. And because it's a dry van trailer, made of aluminum that's only about one-eighth of an inch thick, I doubt it could support our combined weight without buckling a bit. You got a problem with this end?" she asked with a teasing grin.

"No, just need you to school me, that's all."

"Good," she replied; then with quick, efficient movements she made the roof of the truck accessible to them by opening the truck's hood so they could shimmy up on the engine block, step over the windshield and visor. Soon they were sitting on the roof, side by side. The light breeze and bright moonlight made their little spot in the world—the back lot of the grocery store, of all places—all the more enchanting.

C.J. inhaled and exhaled deeply and contentedly. "This is heaven."

She and Ethan linked fingers.

"Much nicer than I'd assumed," he admitted. "When you first mentioned climbing up here I wasn't sure how comfortable it would be."

"So you really like it up here?"

"Yes."

"I've never brought anyone else up here before—not family and certainly no man. This is my special place to come and think. I know it sounds dumb, but I happen to think the stars look better when I'm sitting here," she said with a grin.

"So does this mean I'm special, too?" Ethan asked in a joking tone that belied the seriousness of his question. He expected an answer. A straight one.

"Yes. . . ." C.J.'s answer was decisive but her tone tentative. She realized she was venturing into risky territory, so she added playfully, "You're special, Ethan . . . you *and* Fu Manchu—he's been up here with me, too."

Ethan seemed satisfied with her reply—despite the fact that she'd tacked on that part about the silly sock monkey.

C.J. studied Ethan's face. With her free hand, she tenderly traced his angular jawline. "You're a great guy. A great *friend*."

"Just a friend? C.J., I have to tell you . . . I think I'm falling in love with you."

"But Ethan, we just—"

"I know we just met and you're not sure you believe in love, let alone love at first or second sight. I know how you feel about relationships . . . but when it's right it's right. You just know it . . . in here." Ethan's hand touched the place on his chest near his heart; then he cupped her nape and nudged her closer.

"But . . . I—"

Ethan hushed her. "You don't have to say it back right now. I know that's not what you're feeling . . . yet. When you finally say it, I know you'll not only mean it but will be ready to move ahead with me."

When he gently touched her lips with his, something inside C.J. stirred. The intensity of emotion that suddenly overtook her was too much. She slowly broke the kiss to gaze into his eyes. The sincerity and affection she saw reflected there made her heart flutter.

Just a few short days ago she was determined to make sure she didn't get too emotionally attached to Ethan, but she found her defenses crumbling. Fast. Way too fast. She'd never been in love before, but her gut told her she was well on her way to falling— if she hadn't fallen already. No. Crashed into it like a meteor from space. Could she just walk away after a few more dates? The more time she spent with him, the stronger and deeper their feelings would get. *And this was a bad thing?* Most women would be over the moon about meeting a great catch like Ethan, who actually *wanted* romance, commitment, and love. He was perfect. This made C.J. curious about the marriage Ethan had briefly spoken of that night in Chicago.

"Ethan, you said you'd been married before. What happened? Why did you get a divorce?"

"I didn't get a divorce," he said, his voice dropping low. "My wife, Leigh-Ann, passed away . . . along with our daughter, Hailey."

"What!" C.J.'s eyes went wide. "How?"

"Leigh-Ann and Hailey died in a car accident a little over a year and a half ago," he said slowly as sadness blanketed his handsome features.

"Oh, Ethan, I'm sorry to hear that." C.J. curled an arm around his waist. "Would you like to talk about it?"

Ethan spent the next hour sharing the most painful experience in his life with C.J. She listened intently, then commented and asked questions with compassion and genuine interest. From what C.J. could tell, Ethan had been through an emotional hell and back but had managed to reclaim his will to love and live. He was obviously made of sturdier stuff than she was, but what if he lost someone again? He'd just revealed that he was in love with her. He believed they could build a happy life together. But for how long? He'd opened up to her and now C.J. decided it was time she told Ethan more about her own history.

"I have something to tell you as well that might help you understand why I feel the way I do . . . about commitment, love . . . You know, the man-woman thing."

"Go on." Ethan squeezed her hand encouragingly.

"I'm a cancer survivor. Was diagnosed with Hodgkin's disease at age fifteen and then later a type of blood cancer or leukemia at age nineteen that required a bone marrow transplant."

"Oh, C.J., honey. . . ." Ethan immediately enveloped her in a warm, strong embrace and rocked her for the longest time.

She closed her eyes and allowed the tears that had welled up in her eyes to fall. She let herself get lost in his embrace. It was then she knew for a fact she had fallen head over heels in love with him. She never wanted him to let go, but she knew she'd have to, sooner rather than later—especially in light of what she'd just learned about his wife and child.

Ethan held on, whispering comforting words against her cheek. "Tell me you're fine now. You are, right?"

"It depends on your definition of fine." C.J. withdrew and released a sarcastic snort as she swiped at the tears on her cheeks. "I've been in remission for seven years now."

"Then why are you crying, baby?" He'd held on to her hand, so he kissed it. "That's wonderful. Five years usually means the doctors think you're out of the woods, right?"

"I have routine checkups with my oncologist and other specialists. And I see a family practitioner, who is a family friend, often."

"And you're fine, right?" he repeated.

"True, physically . . . well, doctors tell me I'm OK . . . for now."

"What do you mean 'for now'? Is that what they say to you?"

"The 'for now' part is what I say. Cancer has come to me not once but twice. Who is to say that it won't book a return engagement?"

"Not to make light of your feelings, but who is to say I won't step off a curb tomorrow and get hit by a Mack truck? I mean, I never would've thought I'd lose my wife and my daughter the way I did. Life doesn't come with guarantees, baby, for anyone. That's just not how it works."

"Yeah, but look at the odds. *My* lousy odds so far. I've had to do battle with cancer twice already. *Twice,* Ethan."

"And you won both times. You kicked cancer's ass. You're still here! You're healthy. You look wonderful. You have family, friends, and a man . . . *me* . . . who love you. Life is good to you now. Finally. And you deserve it. I'd think you'd want to embrace that, take all it has to offer . . . live every second to the fullest. Live every day as if it were your last. Have I exhausted all the tired clichés out there yet?" He smiled and attempted to coax a smile out of her. "I'm prepared to roll out a lot more. Whatever it takes! I love you. Did you hear me? I want to drive back to the Dream Cruise and shout it to everyone on the route."

That sounded like something straight out of one of Nina's romance novels. Real corny but at the same time so sweet. So Ethan.

But C.J. just couldn't let go and let loose. The fear was just too old and too stubborn. She stilled herself. She couldn't get carried into Ethan's fantasies for how it could be.

"I didn't mean to be flippant about what you just revealed." Ethan sobered again. "I can't even begin to really know what it feels like to deal with a potentially fatal disease. What I want to focus on is the fact that you're cancer free and that's something to celebrate and fall down on your knees each day and thank the Lord for, but—"

"I *am* grateful." C.J.'s voice rose along with her frustration. "It's complicated, Ethan. I don't always understand my own thought process on this. All I know is I'm afraid of letting my guard down again, getting my hopes up that I can live a normal life only to find out I'm sick again. It doesn't have to be the cancer. It could be a slew of other things."

"Other things?"

"Yes. I can still suffer from some awful and pretty nasty long-term side effects, because of the strong drugs and treatments I had to receive to fight the cancer." She threw up her hands. "Because of some of the radiation treatments I received I'm not even sure if I can have children."

"But you're not sure you can't, either, right?"

She felt herself growing frustrated because she wanted to buy into what he was saying, but she knew that would be a big mistake. "Look, Ethan," she sighed. "I don't want to talk about this anymore. I've told you what I thought you needed to know to understand where I'm coming from on this relationship thing—and I'm thinking . . . I don't know . . . maybe we should cool it a bit for right now."

For Ethan that was like a dropkick in the gut. "What? You don't mean that. Don't shut down on me now. I think it's important that we got all this out so we can move forward. It's been really good between us, hasn't it? You can't deny that."

"Yes, it's been good. But for *how long,* don't you see? I'm sure at some point I *will* drive you nuts, Ethan. Eventually you'll leave skid marks trying to get away from me."

"*If,* big *if* here, if you got sick again, you think I'd just abandon you? Is that it? No way would I ever do that! I'd stay by your side and support you no matter what. That's what love is all about—not just skating through the good times but getting through the difficult times, too. Together."

A sad smile settled on C.J.'s lips. She cupped Ethan's cheek with one hand and saw the sincerity reflected in his eyes. "Oh, Ethan. You would stick by me, wouldn't you?"

"Hell yeah, I would!"

"It just wouldn't be fair to you to have to do that.

And I feel even stronger about this now that I know how much you've already lost—a wife and child. I just couldn't put you through that. You don't deserve that kind of burden *again*."

"Whether I choose to take it on or not is *my* decision. And I'm telling you I *want* to be with you, the whole nine yards, for richer and poorer, till death do us part—"

C.J.'s jaw dropped. "Are you saying what I think you're—"

"Yes! I'd want you to be my wife . . . when you're ready. That should prove to you just how serious I am about sticking with you. We could fly to Vegas, or if you want a long engagement . . ."

C.J. shook her head, utterly flabbergasted by what he'd suggested. "Have you not heard a word I've said? Have you lost your mind? I can't marry you! I just told you that I can't even continue to date you under the circumstances."

"I know it sounds crazy and impulsive, everything is moving fast, but when it's right, it's right. I feel it in here." He held his hand near the place on his chest near his heart.

"Don't say another word. I'm going to show you something." C.J. unlaced one of her Reebok sneakers, then pulled it off. Her white terry sock came off next. She rolled up the edge of her blue jeans to her shin and pointed to one ankle. "See that?"

"What?"

"That big knot there on the inner side of one ankle."

Ethan nodded when he saw the quarter-size knot about an inch from a joint bone. "What is that?" His voice held a note of alarm.

"I'm told it's something called a ganglion cyst."

"A cyst? But I thought you said your health was fine."

"It's harmless, totally benign." She rolled the edge of her jeans back down.

Ethan exhaled, his relief evident.

"I haven't been wearing my favorite black boots the last few days. I'm told I probably had the boots tied too tight and that restricted ankle movement and that caused extra fluid to collect in a little pocket that formed that knot."

"So?"

"It's a perfect example of why I'll never be completely normal. I discovered it about four days ago and imagined all kinds of horrible things. I frantically raced over to have it checked out by Kaye, my doctor."

"So? Lots of people would've reacted the same way if they'd found a suspicious knot on any body part. What's the treatment?"

"Ice and ibuprofen to relieve the discomfort and swelling. If that doesn't work, after a few days Kaye will aspirate with a needle to drain the fluid and then inject a steroid solution."

"Problem solved."

"No, it's not! Don't you see? With me, every headache is a brain tumor and a bad case of heartburn is a heart attack. You'll become exhausted by it all. It's just a matter of time."

"Let me worry about that. OK, so you can get a little neurotic sometimes—"

"A *little* neurotic?"

"So? Look into getting counseling."

"See, you're already thinking I'm a nutcase—as you should. Now let's go, Ethan. I'm really tired." C.J. scooted away to put more inches between them.

"Wait." Ethan reached to latch on to her arm.

"Even if you could handle the wackiness involved with the hypochondria, that doesn't erase the fact that I've had cancer—twice—and there's a good chance I could get it again. If you won't look out for yourself, I have to. You're a wonderful man, Ethan. You can do better. *Way* better, believe me."

"What does that mean?"

"It means I've decided. It's final. I won't see you anymore."

"Oh no, *hell,* no. You're not walking out of my life, C.J. I won't let you."

"There's nothing you can do about it," she said with conviction.

Stunned by her decision, he sat on the hard metal surface and watched her as she avoided his stare.

She moved to climb down from the truck's roof.

Ethan followed. She secured the hood, then made her way to the driver's side of the Barracuda.

"And we can't even remain friends?" Desperation clung to his words.

"Ethan, you just asked me to marry you, remember?" she said wearily as she turned to face him. "Friendship is *not* what you want. And us talking and spending more time together right now is not going to help matters. I'd appreciate it if you didn't phone me or come to my house anymore. We both need space; then maybe later . . . much later . . . when we aren't so emotionally involved, we can reconsider being friends again."

Ethan desperately latched on to what he needed to hear. "So you *are* emotionally involved? You're falling in love, too, aren't you? Aren't you? Say it!" His eyes pleaded and a long minute of silence passed between them.

C.J. swallowed the lump aching in her throat and considered how far she wanted to take the truth. Yes, she truly believed she was falling in love with Ethan. And it had happened so fast it made her head spin. No use resorting to lies when both had been laying all their cards on the table that night. "Yes, I'm falling in love with you, which is why I *have* to let you go." She fought back the fresh tears that threatened to break through. She wouldn't let herself cry again. In time, after he found someone else without all the damn baggage, not only would Ethan understand, but he'd also be grateful that she'd been strong enough for the both of them.

"I knew it! You love me, too!" Ethan's face broke into the widest smile.

"My admitting that changes nothing, Ethan. This won't work."

"It can and it will. We're in love." His smile lingered, growing brighter by the moment.

Fessing up to her true feelings had been a bad move. Big mistake. Now he wouldn't give up. Now she'd have to pull out all the stops and play the cold bitch to get him to back off, no matter how much her heart was breaking. And she thought she'd already experienced it all—as far as excruciating pain went.

"It *will* work," he said.

She backpedaled and stammered, "What I meant was . . . I *think* I might be falling in love with you now, but I don't really know what love is, remember? Maybe it's not love at all . . . what I'm feeling. . . . Maybe it's just simple gratitude."

"Simple gratitude? For the work we've done on the Barracuda?" Ethan chuckled at how ridiculous that sounded.

"No, for accepting me, up to this point. Just the way I am."

"Just gratitude, huh? You *can't* be serious. I'm not buying it. Nice try, though."

"Lust has a lot to do with what I'm feeling, too. The way you made me feel on the hood and in the backseat of this car. It had been a while, a long while, since I'd had sex. Maybe I'm confusing lust and love."

"No, I refuse to believe that. There's more between us and you know it."

"It's over," she said with steely determination. She turned her back to him and jabbed her key in the passenger side door of her Barracuda. "Now get in. I'll drive you home."

"You don't want it to work. You just want to take the easy way out and throw it all away."

"Ethan . . . ," she started, eyelids jammed closed in exasperation. If she wasn't careful he would break her down.

He grabbed her by the shoulders to whirl her around to face him.

She opened her eyes and saw the hard set of his jaw and his flaring nostrils. "You can save the I'm-doing-this-for-you crap because I ain't trying to hear it anymore. I don't need you playing the martyr for me. You love me and I love you. We *will* work it out."

Harsher, she said to herself as she bit out her words. "No, we won't. It's over, Ethan."

"The woman I fell in love with is feisty. She's a fighter. She goes for what she wants and doesn't take no for an answer. She's *not* a coward or Chicken Little, sitting back and waiting for the sky to fall."

Colder, she repeated to herself. "Let me go, Ethan."

"Give it a chance, just one chance," he said in a thick voice that finally cracked with emotion.

C.J.'s heart squeezed in her chest as she read the anguish on his face. She wanted to let go and give in but couldn't. She knew breaking things off was best.

Her hesitation must have given him hope, as he moved closer to kiss her lips, but she merely yanked her head away, then added like a chilly mantra, "One day . . . sooner than you think . . . you'll thank me for having the foresight—"

"C.J., don't do this," he begged.

C.J. felt her resolve crumbling; she'd have to go for the jugular. "Stop clinging to something that's not meant to be," she said in a brutal performance worthy of an Academy Award. "You're looking for Leigh-Ann's stand-in. That's what your impulsive marriage proposal is all about, isn't it? Can't stand to be alone and single? Well, I'm *not* the one, OK?"

Ethan's head snapped back as if he'd been slapped. He dropped his hands from her shoulders and stared at her as if seeing her clearly for the first time.

He looked at her with such hurt, then disgust, she wanted to snatch the words back as soon as she said them. She'd gone too far, tossing his dead wife in his face like that, but she'd finally gotten the desired effect. What she did was for him. Tough love.

Then a heartrending calm descended over him. He'd surrendered. His tall, strong body went slack as if all the fight had fled right after she blurted those nasty words.

"Fine," he said simply. He bit his lip and studied her for a long minute. She couldn't take the crushed look on his face, so she looked away, but kept her expression blank.

She couldn't yield. She couldn't crack.

He went on, "You win, lady. I give up."

"All right, we understand each other, then. Get in. I think I need to go for gas," she said in a feeble attempt to drag the conversation back to normalcy, which was impossible after such a gut-twisting exchange.

She opened the Barracuda and climbed inside as he walked around the car to the passenger's side. She was behind the wheel when she realized he didn't get in. He kept walking toward the entrance of Farelli's Grocery Store.

She scrambled out of the car and called out to him, "Where are you going?" When he didn't reply she tried again. "Ethan, get in the car. This is ridiculous. You need a ride home."

He kept walking, disappearing around the corner of the building.

C.J. decided to wait in the car. He needed some space. She gripped the steering wheel, and the tears she'd held back while breaking things off with Ethan filled her eyes and streaked down her cheeks. Had she done the right thing? *Yes,* she told herself as she reached for her purse on the backseat. She plowed through it to remove tissue to dry her tears. She hated that she had to resort to such behavior, but it was for his own good. Ethan had been gearing up for a long battle of wills.

C.J. sat in the car for about thirty minutes, just waiting for Ethan to emerge. He did when a Yellow Taxi pulled up to Farelli's electronic doors. He climbed inside the taxi's backseat, catching C.J. by surprise. She'd asked him to back off, and that's what he was doing. He wouldn't even accept a ride home from her. Her first impulse was to tail the cab to his house. And try to soften the blow once she got there. But after she apologized for her hurtful words, then what? She decided to leave things be right then. She rested her head against the steering wheel. *It's all for the best,* she repeated over and over in her mind as she sobbed.

20

Weary and depressed, C.J. spent most of the following day in bed, only crawling out of the covers when the doorbell rang around 4.00 p.m.

Her head felt like a boulder, her stomach churned, and her eyes stung from a marathon crying jag. Several times the night before and that morning she'd reached for the telephone beside her bed to end her misery. She wanted to phone Ethan and tell him she'd made a terrible mistake. She did want him in her life, but then that old, unrelenting fear would resurface. How much life did she have left? And what kind of life would he have with someone like her? Why add one more person to the list of loved ones burdened with caring for her when she became too weak and pathetic to care for herself? Why add one more person to leave behind?

C.J. donned her robe and made her way to the front door. She found her parents on the other side.

"Why aren't you dressed yet, girl?" Malcolm said as he stepped inside and wrapped her in his thick, warm arms. "I know you didn't forget. It's the official Dream Cruise night! Ella told us you all had a ball cruising last night, but Friday night isn't nearly as exciting as Saturday night, I hear. Ella says the 'Cuda looks great! Can't wait to see it! You got it in the garage, right?"

Grace then took her turn giving C.J. a hug and kiss on the cheek. "Are you all right?" Her brow pleated with concern as she pressed the back of one hand against C.J.'s forehead. "You look as if you might be coming down with something, dear."

"I'm OK, Mom," C.J. said. "Just didn't get much sleep last night, so I stayed in bed much of the day to try to catch up on the Z's I lost."

"And did you? You've been looking forward to this night for a while. I know you don't want to pass it up," Grace pointed out as she walked to the sofa and sat. Malcolm followed.

Skipping that night's big cruise did cross C.J.'s mind, but if she did, after all the yammering she'd done about it over the years, her parents would know something was wrong. And they wouldn't leave until they got what it was out of her. She didn't want to discuss Ethan and what had happened with them.

"If C.J.'s not feeling up to it and wants to pass on the Cruise, Grace, she can," C.J.'s father said. "Don't pressure the girl."

"Oh, honey." Her mother's hand moved to her mouth. "I didn't mean to sound as if I was pressuring you. Was I pressuring you?"

"You're not pressuring me, Mom, but even if you were, it's OK," C.J. said, cutting off an apology she knew would soon follow.

"It's just that I know how much you've been looking forward to this, that's all. You look so tired, honey. You sure you're not coming down with something?"

"I'm fine. I'm just going to go take a quick shower, brush my teeth, and throw on some clothes. Should be ready in half an hour." C.J. reached for two remote controls, one for the TV and one for her stereo system, then passed them both to her parents so they could entertain themselves in the meantime.

"You sure you're up to this?" Grace asked.

"Yes, I'm sure," C.J. replied.

"Leave the girl alone, Grace," Malcolm said. "And honey, you look beautiful, just beautiful, as always."

With a bad case of bed head, C.J. knew she looked like crap, but her father would never admit that— even when the chemo had destroyed every strand on her head and made her look like a human billiard ball. A small smile played on her lips. Any other time she might have become annoyed at her father's compliment, but she'd done a lot of thinking the night

before. Her attitude as far as her parents were concerned really sucked. OK, they went overboard a lot
of times. They'd laid it on too thick, but there were
worse things than having parents who thought the sun
rose and set because of you. Parents who wanted
nothing more than your good health and happiness.
They weren't perfect and neither was she. Maybe if
she'd just sat down with them to explain what she
needed from them—less sugarcoating, more candor.
Even when it was something they thought she
wouldn't like hearing. She wanted more honesty, but
she hadn't been straightforward with them, either. Instead, she'd brooded, pouted, then brooded and
pouted some more. And when she wasn't doing those
things, she'd behaved like a whiny ingrate. A part of
her had resented her parents all these years because
she just wanted to be treated like an ordinary teen
when everything in her world was far from ordinary.
True, their coddling of her had continued to this day,
but how could she expect them to stop kowtowing to
her as if she were on the verge of keeling over any
minute when she'd always behaved as if she were a
dead woman walking? Her emotions and thoughts
were in a jumble, but she knew she had to try to make
at least one thing right where her personal relationships were concerned. She would finally open up for
once—without the anger or sarcasm but with kind-
ness and tact, she'd let them know how she felt. She
moved to settle on the sofa between them. She

wrapped her arms around both and hugged them close. "Mom, Dad . . ." She drew in a deep cleansing breath. "Before we leave for the Cruise . . . we really need to talk . . ."

People began arriving at the black-tie fund-raising gala around 7:00 p.m. Ethan, along with the rest of the planning committee, who had rented rooms in the hotel for convenience, arrived several hours earlier.

The night kicked off with a silent auction of offerings from jewelry and clothing designers.

A tuxedoed Ethan worked the cavernous hotel ballroom, greeting and schmoozing with the guests who'd paid five hundred dollars apiece to participate in the festivities, which included a four-course dinner, a live jazz band, and dancing. Staying focused was no small feat when Ethan's thoughts kept drifting to that blowup he'd had with C.J. the night before. Her words had cut him to the bone and he was still reeling in the aftermath, but he had a job to do. He was determined to stay in the moment to make sure the evening they'd been planning for months was a huge success. He owed that to Leigh-Ann.

The women on the committee had outdone themselves, he thought, as he scanned the opulent white and silver decor. The tables sparkled with glowing candelabras and vases filled with faux silky daisies, Leigh-Ann's favorite flowers.

"What a fancy shindig," Gus said to Ethan when he finally weaved his way to his grandfather's table. "Good job!"

As Ethan had assumed he would, Gus, who looked distinguished in his midnight blue tux, had brought Ella as his date. She looked stylish and contented in her berry-colored sequined evening gown and matching jacket.

"Everything is lovely, just lovely, Ethan," she said in a bouncy voice that made Ethan assume she knew nothing about his breakup with C.J.

Because Ella and Gus knew C.J. was doing the Dream Cruise that evening, her absence did not seem odd.

"Thank you, but you two be sure to praise Beatrice and Jacinda, in particular, who worked tirelessly to make sure all the details were perfect," Ethan said. "Those two deserve most of the credit."

Jacinda, wrapped in a strapless red evening gown that clung to her petite but voluptuous frame, suddenly appeared to stand beside Ethan. "Did I hear my name?"

"Yes, you did," Gus said. "How are you doing this evening? Long time no see. Good to see you again."

Gus had become acquainted with Jacinda at the many barbecues Ethan and Leigh-Ann had held at their Farmington Hills home.

"It's nice to see you again, too, Gus." Jacinda moved closer to the older man to give him a quick hug.

"This is Ella, my date," Gus said proudly.

Jacinda accepted the hand Ella extended. "Nice to meet you, too."

"I love your dress." Ella smiled. "Back in the day, that sexy little number would've had *my* name written all over it."

"Back in the day?" Gus wrapped his arm around her shoulders and pulled her close. "No offense to Jacinda and the other young fillies in here, but Ella, darlin', you could *still* wear a dress like that and outshine everyone in here."

Ella blushed and playfully poked at Gus's arm. "Stop embarrassing me, filling my head with all your sweet nonsense."

Gus quickly stole a kiss from Ella's cheek, then said to Jacinda, "Ethan here was just telling us that you and Beatrice really went all out. The ballroom looks fantastic. I'm sure Leigh-Ann would've loved it."

"That's so sweet of you to say, Gus." A melancholy note slipped into Jacinda's voice. "I was hoping that we did Leigh-Ann proud. This evening isn't just about raising money, it's a tribute to her."

"Gus told me all about her," Ella said. "Sounds like she was such a lovely person—inside and out."

Before Ethan could comment, John Paul, Leigh-Ann's cousin, who was also on the planning committee, approached the group to let Ethan know it was time to head to the dais to address the guests. Ethan hadn't practiced or scribbled notes for his speech. He didn't have to. He'd planned to speak from the heart about his wife, her dream, and the purpose of the fund-raiser. And that's exactly what he did. When he was done there were few dry eyes in the room. Ethan noticed that Jacinda, who was seated nearby, seemed to have the most trouble collecting herself, which she was still doing long after the speeches and tributes were done.

Everything went off without a hitch, and by the gala's end, about two and a half hours later, more than enough cash had been raised to fund several college scholarships for high school art students.

The ballroom was practically empty save for the hotel staff who had started to clean. Ethan tugged the tie off his neck and loosened the top buttons of his shirt as he ventured out to one of the ballroom's balconies that overlooked the hotel's entrance. He braced his arms against the banister as the warm night air brushed over his skin. He looked skyward and whispered, "We did it, babe."

"Thinking about Leigh-Ann?" Ethan heard Jacinda's voice behind him. "I hope I didn't startle you."

"Yeah, I was thinking about her. And no, you didn't startle me, but I thought you'd already left for your room."

"I had and I went by your room." Jacinda moved to stand beside him. "When I realized you weren't there I figured I'd find you here."

"You went by my room? What's up?"

"I felt Leigh-Ann's presence here tonight. I'm pretty sure she thinks we did good."

"That's a nice thought. You and the committee really worked your butts off."

"Don't sell yourself short, Ethan, you did your part, too. Leigh-Ann would be proud."

"Thanks."

"I'm sure your melancholy mood all night was brought on by your memories of Leigh-Ann and Hailey, too."

Ethan had been thinking about the wife and child he'd lost, but C.J. had also darted in and out of his mind. Her words had been seared into his consciousness: *Leigh-Ann's stand-in. That's what your impulsive marriage proposal is all about, isn't it? Can't stand to be alone and single?*

Had he been in too much of a rush toward matrimony? Was he trying to recapture what he'd had with Leigh-Ann? He'd turned that question over and over again in his mind since he and C.J. parted in the parking lot of Farelli's Grocery Store. He needed to talk about it, to get some perspective, but he refrained from confiding in Jacinda about his woman problems.

"I went to your room because I needed to talk to you . . . to explain some things. I mean, really come clean about my behavior toward you as of late."

"Oh?" Ethan turned and propped his rear against the banister.

"Yes." Jacinda sighed. "I'm sure you think I've

been behaving pretty strange lately. Snapping at you and such."

"Yes, and you've already apologized for that."

"I did." Jacinda nodded. "But I wasn't completely honest and I won't feel right until I get some things off my chest."

"OK." Ethan gestured for her to continue. "I'm listening."

Jacinda looked down at the red pumps on her feet. "I'm not sure where to begin and my thoughts and feelings are in such a mess—"

"It's all right. Take your time." He reached out to stroke her arm.

Jacinda tried to stay focused on Ethan's eyes but quickly looked away as if it were just too hard. "You see, Ethan . . . the thing is . . ." She looked down at her feet again. "I've been riding you so hard lately, questioning your loyalty to Leigh-Ann's memory and judging your mourning period and time line for moving on, because . . ." Her words trailed off.

"Go on."

"Well, I was projecting my own screwed-up emotions on you."

Ethan pleated his brow. "I'm confused . . ."

"I know you must be, because I'm still trying to make sense of it all myself. I've felt lousy and guilt-riddled because I'm the one who hasn't been honoring Leigh-Ann's memory appropriately."

"That's nonsense! Of course you have. Leigh-Ann couldn't have asked for a better friend."

Jacinda released a humorless chuckle; then she tipped her head to look up at Ethan. "Oh, but I beg to differ. A really good friend would not have been coveting Leigh-Ann's husband."

"Coveting her . . . ?" Ethan asked slowly; then when he finally got a clue, he blinked. "What?"

"Lusting after her husband. It started while she was still alive and I went so far as to begin fantasizing about what it would be like to have Leigh-Ann out of the picture."

Ethan shook his head and without thinking he moved to put more space between them. "Jacinda, I—"

"Wait, let me finish. Of course, when Leigh-Ann was alive I never would've acted on it—not to suggest that you would've been tempted anyway. You were a good husband, Ethan. But that didn't stop the yearning and the daydreams. Then when Leigh-Ann died . . . I . . . well . . . I was devastated that I'd lost my best friend, wondered if I'd set some sort of bad karma for her in motion. But then at the same time I wondered what if . . . you and I . . ." She grimaced. "I know it sounds appalling and I'm deeply ashamed of myself, but I just couldn't get a handle on the obsession. Then just recently I started acting on the feelings, trying to keep you involved with Luminesque so I'd always have an excuse to see you and spend time with you."

"Why are you telling me all this and why now . . . tonight?"

"Because I've treated you unfairly. And tonight, when we were doing something to honor Leigh-Ann's memory, seemed perfect. I needed to confess so *I* can move on."

Ethan wasn't sure what to say to her. While Jacinda was a beautiful woman with a lot of other things going for her, he wasn't the least bit interested in hooking up with her *that* way and doubted he'd ever be. While he respected her need to purge, her confession would strain things between them from that night on. He did have one question, however. He thought back to Beatrice's suggestion that Ethan act as Jacinda's escort that night. "Does Beatrice know how you feel?"

"Oh God, no!" Jacinda shivered and hugged herself as the night air got chillier. "At least I didn't tell her anything, not how I was feeling when Leigh-Ann was still alive."

Ethan removed his tuxedo jacket and draped it around her shoulders. "I got this strange feeling that she was trying to play matchmaker, but I could be wrong."

"I suppose it's possible that she was. And I know she fully expects you to move on with your life and she wishes you well. She loves me and she loves you, so there's a chance she was thinking like I was at one point . . . *what if* . . ."

Ethan found that idea disconcerting. His former mother-in-law dipping in his love life and trying to choose women for him. If that, indeed, was what she was doing he'd tell her to back off, though he dreaded having that conversation with her.

"I spend quite a bit of time with Beatrice. If she ever says anything to me directly I'll set her straight, discreetly and gently, of course. Don't worry about it."

"Thank you," was about all Ethan could say.

"No, you shouldn't be thanking me. I know I put you on the spot, but I appreciate your listening and not making me feel awful. You won't have to deal with me anymore."

Ethan tried to put his uneasiness aside to comfort her. "It took a lot of courage to reveal what you just did. I still consider you a friend—"

"You do?"

"Yeah. And if you ever need anything . . ."

Jacinda's eyes filled with tears. "I'm glad to hear that. I do know the right guy is out there for me. I feel as if a fog has lifted. I think I can see my way clear to finding him now."

"And I'm sure you will—wait, I know you will." Ethan moved to encircle her in a hug.

21

As soon as the sun rose the next morning C.J. drove to her aunt Ella's. If she didn't talk to someone and try to sort out the mess she'd suddenly made of her simple life, she'd implode.

"I wish you could've attended that gala last night," Ella said, settling into her favorite lawn chair in her small backyard. "It was so lovely. The food was delicious, the band great. I've never seen so many of Detroit's well-heeled citizens in one place. I guess that's not saying much. I never get invited to those kinda swanky shindigs."

"What gala?" C.J. took the matching chair beside her aunt.

"The one Gus invited me to. You mean, Ethan didn't tell you about it?"

"Ethan hasn't mentioned anything to me about any gala."

"Oh, w-well, um . . . ," Ella stammered. "I just assumed you weren't there because of the Dream Cruise. Maybe that's why Ethan didn't mention it to you. Maybe he didn't want you to feel obligated to attend, knowing how much participating in the Dream Cruise meant to you."

"So Ethan was there?"

"Of course he was. It was a fund-raiser, a scholarship fund-raiser, in honor of his deceased wife." Ella paused to search her memory. "What was her name again? . . ."

"Leigh-Ann."

"That's right. So you do know about her."

"Ethan mentioned that he'd been married before during our trip to Chicago, but I didn't know he was a widower until the night before last." C.J. removed her sneakers and carelessly ran her fingers over the knot on her ankle before she sank her toes in the grass.

"Oh? He sure waited long enough to tell you."

"Well, it's not as if I was champing at the bit to tell him my secrets. We both dropped big bombs that night."

"When you say you dropped one, I'm assuming you told him about the cancer?"

"Yes."

"And how did he react?"

"You've met Ethan; how do you think he reacted?"

"Like he's overjoyed it's all behind you. And how did you respond to that?"

C.J. squirmed in her seat. She let a drawn-out pause stretch between them as her gaze settled on a robust oak tree at the far end of the lawn.

"C.J., what's wrong?" Ella prodded.

C.J. finally spoke. "You've been a pretty darn good aunt to me over the years—especially during the darkest and most challenging times of my life. I'll never forget how often you just dropped everything to drive me to and from a chemo or radiation treatment when Mom and Dad clearly needed a break from it all. And I'll never forget the many times you stayed with me, holding my hand or just being a quiet, comforting presence in my hospital room while I slept. Thanks to Mom, Dad, Nina, and you, I was never alone."

When C.J.'s eyes welled up, so did Ella's. "Oh, chile, that's what family is for." Ella reached over to caress C.J.'s hair. "I've always thought of you and Nina as daughters because Claude and I had never been blessed with our own. It was love at first sight for me as soon as I got a peek at you two that day you were born. I can't imagine loving even my own biological children, if I had them, as much as I loved little Nina and Christina." Ella chuckled through her tears. "Oops, sorry. Make that little Nina and C.J."

"You don't know how much I appreciated not only your love and support, but you never stopped treating me like C.J.—even when I was sick. You got on my case when I'd needlessly cop an attitude or get a bug up my butt about something silly. I know I was a little bitch some days because I was so very enraged at the world . . . and at God for letting me get sick in the first place."

"Oh, baby, as much as we all sympathized, none of us really knew the full extent of what you were going through. But forming a united front to be your rock was our main focus."

"I've been thinking about those days a lot more lately," C.J. revealed. "How they molded me into who I am today. I wonder how different my life would be . . . how different I would be if I'd never gone through it."

"I happen to think you turned out to be a pretty strong, very together young woman." Ella entwined her fingers with C.J.'s.

"It's all an act, Aunt Ella. I'm a big ol' fake, a real phony."

"What in the world . . . ? That's nonsense."

"I'm not as tough and together as I pretend to be. In fact, if you must know, I'm a real head case. You have no idea how screwed up I still feel on the inside. I not only obsess about a cancer relapse, but I still fear the late side effects of all the harsh treatments I received. I'm always imagining that I have all these other horrible diseases, too. It's moved beyond the cancer. Sometimes I think I've literally lost my damn mind. I'll get a bruise and immediately start to think I only have a short time to live. Many single women

my age dream about what their weddings will be
like. What they'll wear. Who'll make the guest list.
Me? I dream about all those things, too, only it's not
a wedding, but a funeral. So when Ethan asked me to
marry him the other night, I totally lost it."

"Ethan asked you to marry him?" Ella's face broke
into a wide smile. "Oh, honey, congratulations!
That's wonderful. He's a good boy."

"Not so fast! I turned him down."

"Do you love him?"

"Yes," C.J. replied in a small voice. "Yes, I do."

"And he obviously loves you, but there's nothing
wrong with a long engagement if you're thinking
things are just moving too fast."

"I turned him down 'cause I can't marry him. Period. And I broke things off completely."

"What?"

"Aunt Ella, he lost his wife and child. He doesn't
need to get saddled with someone like me, someone
with my track record."

Ella's brow pleated with concern. "Track record?
Chile, we're all gonna die someday."

"If I hear one more person say that . . ." C.J. felt
her anger bubbling up.

"I realize I can't even begin to know how you
must feel, to live with the kind of gripping terror
that has such a hold on you, but baby, I do know that
you have to find some way to move beyond it so it
doesn't continue to affect your quality of life. Have
you considered seeking help?"

C.J. shook her head. "Kaye said the same thing, mentioned some childhood cancer survivor support groups and even some counselors to me, but I've never pursued any of it because . . ." She shrugged. "I don't know."

"Maybe you should give them a try. You haven't even given them a chance. It might be good to talk to and befriend other people—not just any survivors' group, but people who've experienced that exact same thing you have. Getting sick when you're a child or teen has to be different from getting ill when you're an adult."

"I didn't think that support group stuff would do any good or be something I could stick to."

"Flitting from pillar to post on the road all the time the way you do would make sessions difficult, but not impossible if it's something you really want to do."

"Work has been a type of therapy. It's weird, you know. When I'm on the road I just feel this freedom. It's as if—"

"You're just running. Is it really about liberation or is it more like a way to turn tail and escape rather than standing firm to deal? I know it might sound as if I'm reaching here, but maybe not remaining in the same place for long periods of time can feel like a way to outmaneuver another illness."

"OK, now I hate to say it, but you're really starting to sound like a talking head on daytime TV, some cuckoo psychobabbling shrink, Aunt Ella." C.J. decided she'd tired of this topic, so she tried to lighten the mood. "Hel-lo! Hel-lo! Who are you and what have you done to my aunt?" C.J. laughed, then rose from the seat to wander to that old tree where her late uncle Claude had hung a rope and big tire for Nina and C.J. to play on when they visited as kids. The swing was gone, but C.J. could still picture it clearly in her mind.

Ella followed, not letting C.J. withdraw. "Maybe I have been watching too much *Oprah* and *Dr. Phil,* but let me say this first, then I'll drop it. Promise."

C.J. rolled her eyes but gestured for her aunt to continue.

Ella placed her hands on each side of C.J.'s face. "Look at me and please try to hear what I'm saying. There's no way around it. Being a cancer survivor will always be a part of who you are, but please, honey, try not to let yourself become completely smothered by that part of your past. Don't become so fixated on it that you start to see yourself only as a former cancer patient instead of as a beautiful multifaceted young woman who just happened to have had cancer. You have so much to live for. Do you understand?"

"Yes." C.J. nodded.

"Good." Ella moved her hands from C.J.'s face. "Now about Ethan, I'm just gonna come on out and say it, with no pussyfooting around what's obvious."

"You wouldn't be Aunt Ella if you, what did you call it, pussyfooted? And that's one of the many reasons I love you."

"You know I don't suffer fools gladly." Ella planted one hand on her hip and wagged a finger at C.J. with the other. "If you let that man get away you're a straight-up fool—no ifs, ands, or buts about it. You'd be a fool who needs a good swift kick in the ass." She lifted one sneaker-shod foot off the ground. "And I'm prepared to volunteer my size seven-and-a-half for the job."

"I don't know . . . I said some really messed-up things to him."

"So apologize. Do whatever is necessary to make things right."

C.J. managed a wan smile, though still trying to decide if there would or should be a next move for her where Ethan Tanner was concerned.

22

Dusk had settled when Ethan finished cutting the grass in Gus's backyard. Helping him with yard work had been a weekly ritual for Ethan since his junior high school days. Though he could afford to hire professional help to tend to the landscaping around the two-story brick home where his grandparents had raised him, Ethan liked doing it himself. Now that he lived in a loft and had no lawn of his own to maintain, taking care of Gus's meant even more to Ethan.

Even as a teen Ethan never saw the lawn work as a chore. He found the steady droning of the lawn mower and the repetitive motion of pushing it back and forth, along the expansive front and backyards relaxing. It helped him blot out the rest of the world

so he could think—even meditate and pray. Lawn
work at the Tanner residence also provided yet another enjoyable family bonding activity for him and
his grandparents. When Ethan finished the grass, he
often ventured over to help Gus edge the front lawn
or shape the voluminous hedges that flanked the
front porch. When Gran was alive she would fuss
over the psychedelic ring of annuals and perennials
that circled the house before she disappeared inside.
She'd often return with homemade brownies and
cookies, tall drinking glasses, and a frosty pitcher of
fresh-squeezed lemonade. There were times Ethan's
tender memories of his grandmother—along with
the relentless heat—would conjure up an image of
Gran, standing in the back doorway, calling out to
him and Gus.

That early evening it was so hot and humid,
Ethan had tugged off his T-shirt and cut the lawn
bare-chested. As he left neat strip after strip of
shorn grass in his wake, he thought about his proposal to C.J. and the breakup that followed. Maybe
he had pushed too hard, which had been a bad move
for someone who had so much emotional baggage to
unload. He'd been pushing from Day One. He'd
scared the poor woman shitless; no wonder she'd
lashed out at him the way she had. What had he expected? Maybe he had tried to make too much happen too soon. Her accusation, however, had forced
him to examine his motivation for popping the question so soon. He turned off the mower and made his

way to Gus, who was taking a break from the hedges and relaxing on the top step leading to the back door.

Ethan reached for his T-shirt and used it to wipe the sweat from his face and neck. He planned to spend the night, so he'd borrow one of Gus's old T-shirts for the drive home the next morning.

Gus passed him one of the chilled cans of beer he'd retrieved from the fridge. "It's not your Gran's lemonade, but it'll have to do."

Ethan accepted the offering, popped the tab, and upended the can to take several thirsty gulps.

He drank so long and hard that when he finally pulled the can away from his lips he'd almost drained it.

Gus eyed him curiously. "Damn. You need something much stronger? Got some vodka in the house and some empty pickle jars big enough to dive in and backstroke." He chuckled. "You all right?"

Ethan exhaled, swiping the back of his hand across his mouth. "What would you say if I told you I asked C.J. to marry me?"

"You what?" Gus's eyes bucked.

"I asked her to marry me. Friday night. After you and Ella took off with Betsy Blue for your stroll along the river. C.J. and I spent some time together away from the cruise, and then I . . . well . . . I popped the question. I hadn't planned on it. It just came out and it seemed so right at that moment when I was trying to convince her that I'd never abandon her. That if she gave us a chance, she could trust me to stand by her no matter what."

"So what did she say?"

"She broke things off," Ethan muttered, looking across the lawn at nothing in particular.

"Damn, not what you were expecting, I'm sure."

"See, she's got all these reservations, one of which involves Leigh-Ann and Hailey."

"How so?"

"Because I lost Leigh-Ann and Hailey the way I did." He maneuvered his long frame to face Gus. "Granddad, I'm going to ask you something and I need you to be brutally honest."

"OK, shoot."

"She said something about my just looking for a stand-in or substitute for Leigh-Ann, as if I can't stand not being married. As if any warm and ready body will do. That was a particularly low blow."

"Well, you *were* a very happily married man."

Ethan shot the older man an angry look. "Not you, too."

"All I said was that you loved being married; you thrived in that relationship."

"True, my years with Leigh-Ann and my baby were the best, but if I were just looking for anyone to plug into their empty spaces I would've hooked up with someone long before now. It has been a year and a half and it's not as if I haven't had lots of opportunities."

"You got that right. Some of those young ladies

down at the church could barely contain themselves to give you a respectable mourning period."

"But beyond that, the bottom line is there *are* no substitutes for Leigh-Ann and Hailey. And I resented what she said like hell. Besides, Leigh-Ann and C.J. are as different as night and day."

"Yup. Is it possible that C.J. doesn't even believe that mess herself? That you're just trying to rush back into marriage simply because you like being part of a legally bound unit. You know, maybe she was just looking for excuses to mask her real reasons for rejecting your proposal."

"Yeah, actually, I'm pretty sure she said what she did just to push me away . . . for my own good."

"For your own good?"

"Yes." Ethan sighed. "It's a long story."

"I've got time."

Ethan spent the next hour filling in Gus on C.J.'s background.

"Oh, I get it now," Gus said after taking a reflective moment. "The poor girl is scared."

"Yeah."

"But you're not going to give up on her, are you?"

"I just don't know. I love C.J., but I feel as if I've been pushing this thing with her from Day One. This is something she's going to have to work through for herself. *She's* got to want to conquer it and move it forward."

"And when she does—"

"You mean *if* she does."

"All right, *if* she does, will you be there for her?"

"Only time will tell, Granddad, only time will tell."

23

When Monday rolled around, C.J. was glad she had two runs scheduled. She had a job that would take her to Nashville. The plan was to run down south to deliver a load of car batteries, then return to Detroit immediately for another load—bottled water—to be hauled to Chicago. Both jobs provided perfect opportunities to put some distance between herself and her problems for several days.

Before C.J. hit the road, she'd dropped Pryde and Joi off at Ella's place. She was taking over cat-sitting duties because Nina had yet to return from New Orleans.

The drive to Nashville seemed longer and lonelier than usual because C.J. had Ethan on the brain. She'd left Detroit city limits around 3:00 p.m., then encountered lots of highway construction and clogged traffic. By the time she'd delivered her load to the designated location it was late or rather very early the next morning. She didn't pull into her favorite Nashville-area chew and spew, aka truck stop/diner, until 2:14 a.m.

She drove under the fuel island, which housed about a dozen pumps. Though the temperature had soared to a sweltering ninety-eight degrees, she reached in the back of the cab for the old cotton jacket to cover her T-shirt, then donned unlined leather gloves for her hands. Diesel burned if splashed or dribbled on the skin. She checked to make sure the nozzle was off. Occasionally an asshole trucker would leave the nozzle turned on, so when the next trucker picked it up diesel fuel would spray everywhere. As C.J. was filling the left tank, she felt as if she was being watched. She scanned the area, which had three other truckers refueling. Her gaze landed on a tall potbellied guy with a thick handlebar mustache and baseball cap. His eyes were shielded by dark shades. *To filter the island's bright lighting?* C.J. wondered, then shrugged it off as she moved to refuel the right tank. She met some strange people in her line of work.

She paid at the pump but would have to collect her receipt inside the little store connected to the island. First, she needed to find a parking slot for the night. The area was packed with rows of trucks. She estimated that there were about a hundred of them.

C.J. worried that she wouldn't find a space, but soon she spotted two spaces near the far end of the lot, roughly one hundred yards away from the store, restaurant, and shower area.

Though she was mentally and physically beat, she quickly and expertly parked her rig in a slot. As she removed her jacket and leather gloves she noticed that another rig had backed up to hers, which was standard procedure.

She'd climbed down from the cab and secured its locks when she took a step back into another body. Startled, she whirled around to see the mustachioed guy who was wearing the dark sunglasses earlier. The shades were gone and now she got a good look at his bloodshot peepers.

"Excuse me," she said, trying to skirt him.

"You didn't say 'sorry,'" he slurred with hot alcohol on his breath.

"Sorry," C.J. said as courteously as possible just to avoid an angry confrontation. She attempted to walk around him again.

He blocked her path. "What's your hurry, honey?" he said with a leer that racked her from head to toe. "I'm parked right behind you. I've got a bottle of Johnnie Walker Red in my truck. What do you say you come back with me so you can apologize to me right proper and we can get to know each other a little better?"

Whatever he had drunk had made him bold enough to harass her, but he wasn't so inebriated that he wasn't a physical threat. For the first time while on a run C.J. was afraid. She considered screaming but didn't know how far the creep planned to take his little intimidation game. She'd feel foolish if it turned out he was just being a jerk and not actually dangerous.

"Take a hike, dude," C.J. said in a take-charge manner. She stiffened her spine as if to indicate that she'd brook no BS.

"Oh, a feisty little thing," he said with a hard glint in his eyes. "I like that. You're just my type; now you have to come to my cab to have a drink with me. I'm insisting," he grunted, suddenly slamming her against her truck so hard it knocked the wind out of her. Before she knew it, one of his grimy hands was mashed against her mouth to muffle her scream and the other had pinned one of her hands to her back.

She chomped into his nasty grease-stained hand as if it were a T-bone steak, but he wouldn't let go. She struggled to knee him in the groin like she'd learned in her class, but he maneuvered his thick legs between her thighs.

Think, C.J., think! But her mind had gone blank as far as her Krav Maga went. All that useless boasting she'd done about knowing it. Foolishly, she hadn't practiced it since she'd taken a refresher course a few months ago, so neither the newest movements she'd learned, nor the old ones, were second nature to her. Her attacker's hand moved from her mouth to put pressure around her neck. She gagged and choked but couldn't force out a scream. Her head got lighter. The sky above blacker. She couldn't go out like that.

24

Despite the heat rushing to C.J.'s face, she managed to keep her head clear and panicking to a minimum.

She wasn't too disoriented to forget—

Yes!

Suddenly the creep backed away from her as a sharp *hummpft!* spewed from his mouth.

With her freed hand C.J. had managed to pick her switchblade from the back pocket of her jeans. She had the knife, with its blade retracted, nudged hard against his groin. His grip around her neck loosened. She coughed and wheezed, but she could speak.

C.J. rammed harder to show that she meant business and bit out through clenched teeth, "Feel that, asshole? It's a switchblade. A really big one. Now let me go and step off or I'm gonna lop off the center of your universe."

The pop-eyed fool paused as if he had the luxury of considering his options. As if he was wondering whether he was quick and strong enough to separate her and her weapon.

At that moment C.J. felt like Dirty Harriet. She was indestructible. In control. She almost wanted him to test her. Give her a reason to skewer his member like a Ball Park frank over a campfire. She increased the pressure against his groin. "One flick . . . just one flick of my wrist . . ."

He finally released her, then had the audacity to chuckle and try to play it off. "I was just teasing you, having fun . . . But I probably got a little too rough and took the game too far."

Game? Was he crazy?

"Had one too many shots, if you know what I mean." He winked. "You know how it is. Some bitches like it rough. Meant no harm."

C.J. gritted her teeth. The pain radiating from her butt to her shoulder blades after he slammed her flush against the truck said otherwise. He was buzzed *and* full of bull. But her switchblade obviously sobered him up—quick, fast, and in a hurry.

He'd had the nerve to bow with a flourish before he moved out of the way to let her pass. C.J. backed away quickly, wielding her switchblade like a hot torch that lit her way. She didn't take her eyes off him until she'd put a safe distance between them;

then she turned and took off for the diner at a sprint. She was definitely going to report that creep, drunk or no, to the authorities. Who knew how many other women he'd harassed?

It was only after she'd entered the diner that she realized that all she had was a description of him and his rig. But she'd seen lots of guys who looked exactly like him at truck stops. His rig also wasn't all that distinctive. She needed a license plate number. She told James Earl, the burly diner manager, whom she'd become acquainted with during her previous Nashville runs, about the encounter.

"Is that joker still out there?" he said with fists drawn tight.

"He was a minute ago. I need to get his license plate number."

James Earl agreed to escort her back out to the lot while he ordered Patsy, one of the waitresses, to phone the cops.

"What did he look like?"

When C.J. described him, James Earl's jaw dropped. "Oh man, C.J., you don't know how lucky you are."

"What?"

"That sounds like that maniac they've been trying to catch for the past four months now. Hey, Doreen, yank that flyer over there on the corkboard."

Doreen, Jame Earl's significant other and the cashier, did as he asked and gave the flyer to him. He passed it to C.J. It was a police artist's sketch. It had two faces—one with the dark sunglasses and one without them. And just as James Earl suspected, it was the man C.J. had encountered. She felt dizzy and her knees wanted to buckle, but she held herself together.

With round eyes and a dry throat, C.J. croaked, "That's him. That's him. No doubt about it."

"He's hit four truck stops and gas stations along I-65 already, but most of his victims have been female gas station attendants and lot lizards."

"Lot lizard" was what some trucker types called a prostitute who hung around truck stops.

"All four were beaten and brutally raped, but one was found dead at an interstate restroom," James Earl added. "She'd been strangled."

C.J. gasped and muttered, "Oh hell, no." She knew people were presumed innocent until proven guilty in a court of law, but she couldn't help lamenting that missed opportunity to make the world a safer place for women by castrating that asshole.

C.J., Patsy, and James Earl left the diner and stalked to the parking area. With C.J.'s switchblade, Patsy's baseball bat, and James Earl's handgun, C.J. believed they could take the creep if he tried to escape or started acting like a damn fool before the cops arrived. She hadn't realized that a band of truckers trailed them; all looked tough and ready to throw down, fisticuffs-style, if needed. But when the slot where his rig had been parked came into view, they found it vacant. They looked toward one of the exits and saw his rig rolling out of the lot. C.J. and James Earl raced in that direction to get his license plate number, but the jerk had obviously removed the plates. *Damn!*

Once back inside the diner, C.J. claimed the back booth. She had to suck in slow, deep breaths to steady her racing heart rate. The cops who arrived questioned her for a good half hour and took her contact information, but didn't require her to go down to the station.

After they departed, James Earl came over to check on her. "Sorry about all that. I know you must be pretty shook up. Dinner's on the house. Order anything you want."

"I can't eat right now, James Earl," she said, her voice barely a whisper. "My gut's in knots. I think I might hurl."

"You're staying overnight, right?" he asked, sliding into the booth next to her and wrapping an arm around her shoulder. "You want an Alka-Seltzer or something?"

"No, I'll be fine, but I'm thinking I might go to a hotel."

"In case that psycho comes back? He'd be a damn fool to show his face around this stop again."

"Yeah, you're probably right."

"But I understand your hesitation to stay here tonight."

"I don't know. I might still stay here."

"Whatever you do, at least take something to eat

with you in case you get hungry later on and don't feel like trekking back to the diner all alone. I'll get Patsy to pack up the day's special for you to carry out."

"Thank you," C.J. said with a weak smile.

Only after James Earl felt confident that C.J. was feeling better did he leave to attend to another customer who beckoned him.

While waiting for her order C.J. went to the restroom. She stood before the smudged mirror and stared at her face, which looked pale and haggard. Her eyes felt like pumice stones, and each tooth felt as if it were wearing a tiny angora sweater. She relieved herself, then went back to wash her hands and splash cold water on her face. Back at her booth, she studied the faces of other truckers in the brightly lit diner. Black, white, Latino. Young. Middle-aged. Old. All male at that time of the morning, which wasn't that unusual. The clock on the wall read 3:10 a.m. A few men ignored her. Two or three whispered among themselves, then eyed her unsympathetically and as if she were an alien from some far-flung planet when they realized she was one of them. It was obvious they thought she'd asked for it—whatever "it" would have turned out to be. And that she was in way over her head and what happened to her would've never happened to a male trucker. *Well, screw you, too!* she thought with a smirk, squelching the urge to give them the finger. She didn't need any more trouble that night.

The group of truckers who had joined her, James

Earl, and Patsy to form a united front in the parking lot had come over to slap C.J. on the back, spout "way-ta-gos," and commend her for her courage. They made her feel welcomed and respected in what was still a mostly male club, though the number of lady truckers had increased significantly over the last decade.

She drew in more deep, calming breaths. With heavy eyelids she rested her folded arms and head on the table. She replayed the encounter with that sexual predator. No doubt she'd been terrified but managed to remain cool in the face of danger. No telling what would've happened to her if she'd let fear get the best of her as it had routinely the last few years. Her survival instinct had kicked into overdrive with that creep in a split second when she didn't really have time to think too long. She realized that she still had a lot of living to do. *Real living.* Not the reasonable facsimile or the going-through-the-motions crap that she'd been guilty of for years.

That night she realized that she'd been through too much where her health was concerned and persevered only to let some deranged beer-bellied sorry excuse for a human being snatch it all away. No way, Hosea! For once, she not only felt but also reveled in an overwhelming sense of empowerment, optimism, and hope for her future. She could truly face down *anything* . . . and win! She could be strong, confident, *and* fight back if needed.

Why had it taken her so long to realize that? She'd wasted so much precious time with a truly screwed-up attitude. She had people who loved her. A good business. A nice home. She had hobbies and interests that gave her joy. *And* she had her health. As Ethan had said and learned—after losing his wife and child—no one was promised tomorrow. An image of that beautiful man flashed through her mind. She had him to love; whether it was for ten days, ten weeks, or ten decades, she was going to take what Ethan had offered to her and relish every single second with him . . . with gusto. That is, *if* he still wanted her. Especially after she'd showed her natural ass and done her damnedest to make life with C.J. sound like a one-way ticket on the Hell Express. Would he even want to give her a second chance?

Patsy came over with a brown grease-stained paper bag and a tall Styrofoam cup. "It's a cheeseburger, fries, and a slice of apple pie. Wasn't sure what you drink, so the cup is empty."

"No, for once, Patsy girl, my cup is quite full," C.J. replied with hard-won clarity.

Patsy gave her a befuddled look.

C.J. tried to explain, "You know that ol' saying about perception? How you view the world with the glass as the metaphor? The glass is half-empty or half-full?"

"Ummmm, yeee-ah. I suppose." Patsy drawled, obviously thinking C.J. was still dazed from the rush of adrenaline brought on from tangling with a homicidal maniac. "The soda fountain is that way." She pointed in the direction of the counter. "Coke, Sprite, Mountain Dew. You can get crushed ice and fill 'er up anytime when you're ready."

C.J. accepted the bag and the cup. "Thank you. I'm just going to sit here for a few more minutes."

"Take all the time you need, hon," Patsy said, patting C.J. on the shoulder. She then moved along to take other customers' orders.

The longer C.J. sat and ruminated, the more she realized that waiting until daybreak in Nashville was not what she wanted. She'd caught her second wind along with another punch of adrenaline. She wanted—*no, needed*—to get back on the road to Detroit. To get back to her family . . .

And Ethan.

She got up and moved to the counter, where Doreen stood behind a cash register.

"Do you have bottled soft drinks?" C.J. removed her wallet from her back pocket.

"Sure do," Doreen replied. "James Earl says your money ain't good here tonight, darlin'."

"I'm gonna need about four bottles of Mountain Dew. Also fill this up with coffee." C.J. placed the Styrofoam cup on the counter. "I'm going to need all the caffeine I can get for the drive back to Detroit." She'd decided she'd deal with the inevitable muscle twitches that would follow. While they were harmless, they were annoying. But she decided the caffeine transfusion was for a good cause.

"You've decided to leave . . . now?" James Earl asked.

"I'm ready to hit the road, do it to it, get the hell outta Dodge."

"I'll walk you to your rig."

"Thanks," C.J. said as he escorted her out of the diner and carried her bags of food and drinks.

At the driver's side door of her rig, C.J. and James Earl embraced.

"Thank you, for everything," C.J. said, her voice thick with emotion. "The way you and the gang in there were ready to fight for me. I'm genuinely touched. I've heard some of the old-timers speak of it, but I didn't think truckers and truck-stop folk shared that kind of camaraderie or got-your-back mentality anymore."

"Hey, girly, I knew you were good people from the giddyup, when you first strutted up in my diner— all piss and vinegar with that attitude of yours. You wore a boyish hairstyle and had no butt to speak of. You're slender now, but you weren't big as a minute back then. Doreen didn't know whether to laugh or whip your ass."

The two shared a long laugh.

C.J. had still been new to the trucking business and had only been in remission for a few months. But James Earl and the diner bunch didn't know her appearance was not some deliberate fashion statement. Her hair had just started to grow back after the chemo. Some people's weight actually soared with treatment, but C.J. had dropped pounds from all the purging she did. A side effect of the powerful cancer-fighting drugs she'd had to take.

"Yeah, I was somethin' back then. Still all mad at the world and determined not to let anyone in."

"Ah, but I saw past the front. What was it? Like six years ago?"

"Seven," C.J. replied.

The two friends shared another hug.

"You take care now." James Earl watched her open the passenger side door, then climb inside. He passed the bags to her.

C.J. waved good-bye at James Earl, started the engine, and pulled out of her slot. It was then she felt a jerk and heard a loud thud.

James Earl ran to the window, waving his hands and pointing to the back of her rig. In her rearview mirror she saw it. She moved a few yards, but the trailer had detached and fallen from the truck. She cut the engine and sprang out of the truck. "What the hell . . . ?" she muttered as she went to inspect the trailer.

"Looks as if somebody reached under the fifth wheel and released your kingpin, darlin'," James Earl said.

"Shit!" C.J. hissed, and stomped her foot. That sort of thing happened often at truck stops, but it had never happened to her. All smart drivers made a habit of checking their fifth wheel every time they left their rigs unattended. But she'd been so distracted by all the drama that morning, doing a check had slipped her mind.

Sometimes a driver with a beef against another driver or the company he or she worked for would pull that sort of stunt. It was costly and embarrassing to call a crane to come lift the trailer so it could get hooked up again. It didn't take C.J. or James Earl long to deduce who'd done that to her rig in retaliation. That psycho.

"Sorry, C.J.," James Earl said slowly. "It sure hasn't been your day, has it?"

C.J. slammed her eyelids closed and forced herself to count to ten. Then she'd muttered, "I'm too blessed to be stressed. Too blessed to be stressed," over and over until she believed it again. She had a new attitude. This was annoying as hell but, in the grand scheme of things, fairly inconsequential. "I can't call a crane until daybreak. Looks as if I'm staying here for a while longer after all," she said in a resigned tone. "I dumped my load already, so at least I don't have to worry about someone stealing that while I'm away. I'm just gonna bobtail on over to a motel to rest."

"Oh no, you won't. You're welcome to stay with me and Doreen," James Earl said, checking his watch. "Her shift is over in thirty minutes. You can leave with her then. You should be with friends right now."

"Thanks," C.J. said with a weary smile. "Maybe it's for the best. That I have to stay, I mean." She was bone tired and her driving wasn't safe for her or other drivers, caffeine or not. When she'd decided she had to get back to Detroit and Ethan, all other rational thought had fled. Nothing short of an under-the-hood disaster or what had happened with the detached trailer could've kept her here.

She just hoped that Ethan accepted her apology and took her back when she returned home. She spent several hours of the night praying for just that.

25

With her trailer back on her bobtail where it should've stayed, C.J. hit Detroit city limits around rush hour. After finally catching a long nap at James Earl and Doreen's place and driving from Nashville only making necessary bathroom stops, it felt as if she couldn't get to Ethan fast enough. She considered taking her rig to Farelli's first to pick up her Dakota. But she decided driving all the way to that lot and then heading to Ethan's shop from there was just too long to wait. Stopping at traffic lights had her squirming in her seat.

"C'mon! C'mon!" C.J. chanted impatiently, willing green to chase the red away.

When she finally got to Tanner's Auto Repair and

Body Shop she parked and practically leaped out of the rig and raced inside, looking for Ethan.

"He took the day off," Sid told her.

A dejected C.J. raced back to her rig. She fished out the business card with Ethan's address scribbled on the back, checked one of the maps she kept in her rig, then wheeled it to his Royal Oak loft in record time. Because of the narrow street, she had to park at a grocery store several blocks away. *No problem,* she thought, actually breaking a sweat as she sprinted toward his building. When she lifted her hand to press the button for Ethan's loft she noticed that the underside of her forearm was flaming red. Her breath caught. "What the . . . ?" She managed a gasp as she examined the area, running a finger over a big swatch of bumpy, inflamed skin. "It's nothing, C.J.," she said firmly, not allowing herself to get weirded out as usual over a little rash. Though she genuinely appreciated Doreen and James Earl's hospitality, the couple was in dire need of a good exterminator. C.J. had never seen so many UFOs with wings and creepy crawly things in one home in her entire life. Something must have bitten her while she was sleeping and now she was having a mild allergic reaction. Whatever the case, she'd slap on some Neosporin—*later*. Right then, she had to get to Ethan.

Anxiously shuffling her weight from one black boot to the other, she pressed the button for his loft but got no answer. She kept that up for several minutes but still got no answer. He either wasn't home or had decided he didn't want any visitors.

C.J.'s shoulders slumped as she made her way back to her rig; she perked up again when she thought about Gus. Maybe Ethan was at his grandfather's place. If not, Gus might know where to find him. She pulled her cell phone out of her purse and called directory assistance, but Gus Tanner's phone number was not listed. "Damn!" C.J. grumbled, but was undeterred. "Surely her aunt Ella would have Gus Tanner's phone number and address. C.J. dialed her cell phone and when Ella answered after the second ring, flopped back in the driver's seat. "Thank God. Aunt Ella? I need Gus's phone number. Pronto!"

"He's right here; I can put him on the phone if you like," Ella said.

"He is? Bless you! Yes! Put him on!"

The next thing C.J. knew, Gus Tanner's affable voice was at her ear. "Hey! What can I do for you?"

"I'm looking for Ethan," she said breathlessly. "Sid told me he was taking the day off. Now I'm at his loft, but he's not answering."

"That's because he's at my place. In the garage, actually, tinkering with my lawn mower, refilling it with gas and sharpening the blades. He cut my lawn for me yesterday. Did a real good job, too. Got my grass in order. See, I was starting to have some real problems with grubs and all on the west side of the house and Ethan—"

"Gus, what's your address?" C.J. hated to be rude and cut off the old man, but she could tell he was gearing up for a long-winded spiel about yard work.

"Oh, I'm sorry, honey. I live on 43523 Honeywell in Lathrup Village. You coming over?"

"Yes, but don't tell Ethan, please." C.J. didn't want to give him a chance to bolt or order her not to come. If he no longer wanted to have anything to do with her, he was going to have to tell her to her face.

"I won't say a word to spoil the surprise." Gus snickered. "I happen to know he's going to be glad to see you."

"You think?" C.J.'s eyes filled with hopeful tears.

"I know. Now get your butt over here and make things right with that boy. He still loves you."

"He does?" C.J. managed around the lump in her throat. "Oh, Gus, thank you. I needed to hear that. I promise I'll never hurt him again."

C.J. ended the call and tossed the cell phone back into her purse as she started the engine of her truck again. Half an hour later she'd navigated the truck down Honeywell. She quickly found the house when she spotted Ethan's Betsy Blue and Ella's Camry.

C.J. climbed from the truck and tried to rehearse how she wanted to apologize to Ethan. Everything that came to mind seemed so inadequate. As soon as C.J. reached the edge of the driveway, she and Ethan caught sight of each other. Wearing a grease-stained shirt, Ethan emerged from the garage. When C.J.

noticed that his expression was hard her heart dropped to her belly and her steps slowed; then she stopped a few yards away. But she wasn't going to wimp out after all that racing to get there. She had to tell him what was in her heart; then and only then could he cuss her out and demand that she leave his granddaddy's property.

"Ethan . . . ," she said in a tentative voice. "I love you and . . . and I want to give us a chance . . . if you still want me. I'm so sorry for all the things I said that night at Farelli's, but if you'd just—"

"Come here," Ethan said with outstretched hands and a smile that broke through like the sun in the aftermath of a storm.

He didn't have to tell her twice. C.J. ran to him and launched herself into his arms, then wrapped her legs around his long, lean torso. "Oh, Ethan, I love you! I love you! I do! I do!" She pressed staccato kisses all over his face, and the music that was his laughter made her soul dance.

He spun her around until she felt downright dizzy with contentment.

When they stopped with the blissful silliness, he set her on her feet and simply whispered, "And you know I love you, too." Heartfelt intensity gleamed in his dark eyes. "And only you, for who you are and what we can do together. I want to marry you because of you, not because of some twisted desire to recreate something that was beautiful while it lasted but is no more."

"I know. . . . Ethan, when I said that stuff about your trying to find a—"

Ethan placed a finger to her lips to silence her. "We don't have to go there again. Things were said in the heat of a disagreement. Forgotten."

"But I know I still have some things to conquer and some old habits and thoughts that won't be purged overnight. I'm willing to do whatever is necessary to get over those hurdles. I'm finally willing to do the hard work now."

"And that's all I need to know," he said, still holding her tight.

It was then that their lips met for a long, deep kiss, which heralded their new beginning together.

"Oh, I think I'm going to cry," Aunt Ella wailed from the front porch, dabbing at her eyes with the edge of her apron. "This is so romantic!"

Gus had enveloped her in a hug. "Oh, honey, we can't let those young-uns have all the fun." He took that moment to ease down gingerly on one knee. He pulled a ring out of his pocket, kissed it, and added with a wheezy snicker, "Now, if this bad back and bum knee go out on me at once and I can't get up, just remember, I got the paramedics on speed dial."

Ella's mouth gaped open and her hand flew to her ample chest. "Oh, Gus!"

"Ella, will you marry me?" Gus said as, stunned and delighted, Ethan and C.J. looked on.

"Yes!" Ella squealed, bending to smother Gus in hugs and kisses.

"Way to go, Granddad!" Ethan shouted.

"You, too, Aunt Ella," C.J. chimed in.

"But we can't let you old folks beat our time," Ethan said to C.J. in a mock conspiratorial tone. "You are going to marry me, too, right?"

"Of course!" C.J. replied. "We'll sit down, talk, and set the date together."

"Hey, Ethan, thought you were so desperate to get to the AutoZone before it closed to get that car part," Gus teased as he slowly rose to both feet again.

"AutoZone? My kinda place!" C.J. cheered.

Ethan moved toward Betsy Blue, climbed inside, then started the engine. He gave C.J. an adoring smile that melted her from the inside out.

"I'm getting ready to ride off into the sunset, lady," he told her with a wink. "Care to join me?"

C.J. finally believed that the fairy tale was possible for a brassy, style-challenged, gear-headed hypochondriac like her.

She hopped inside the truck, smiled back at him, and sighed. "I thought you'd never ask."